Cozy Up to Murder

a novel about a record store,
a cat, purple hats, and murder

by Colin Conway

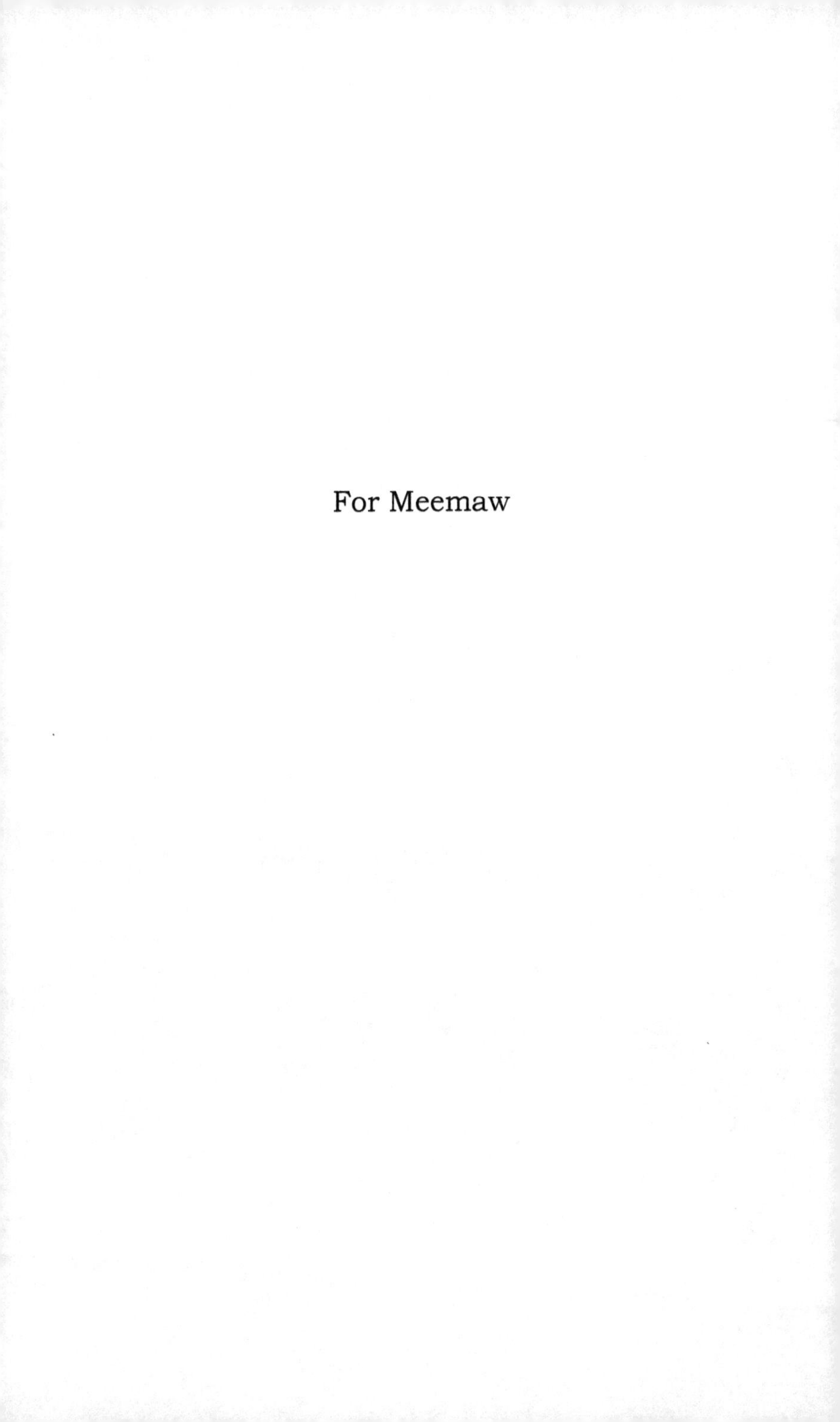

For Meemaw

Booger!

Dr. Johnny Fever
(played by Howard Hessman)/
WKRP in Cincinnati

Chapter 1

The door opened, and a cool breeze rushed in, bringing the aroma of the Pacific Ocean with it. A partially naked man stood in the store's entry.

Deeply tanned, the rotund visitor wore colorful board shorts, flip-flops, and nothing else. A long, twisted braid of gray hair hung over his left shoulder. A ratty beard descended over a puka shell necklace and down to his hairless chest.

Behind the store's sales counter, Owen Hunter stood on a ladder, a rolled poster in his hand. He paused for a moment to study the potential customer.

It's too cool outside to dress like that, Owen silently mused.

As the visitor scanned the store, he rubbed his belly. He nodded in time with the hard rock music playing through a set of hanging speakers.

When his gaze landed on Owen, the man waved and stepped farther into the store. He stopped suddenly, though, and tilted his head as if truly noticing the music for the first time.

His gaze once again swept across the store.

To Owen, it seemed apparent this was not the visitor's first time to Rockafellers, Costa Buena's only used record store celebrating rock and roll of the fifties and early sixties.

The half-naked man's attention passed over posters of Buddy Holly, Jerry Lee Lewis, and Fats Domino. He quickly appraised the shelves of memorabilia dedicated to the early days of rock and roll. When he looked at a speaker hanging in the corner of the ceiling, his brow furrowed.

"What are you playing?" the man asked.

"Music," Owen said, turning to face a back wall covered in monochrome photos and vintage concert flyers. He lifted the rolled poster, exposing enough of it to stick a pin in the upper right corner.

"Not the *right* music."

Owen next pushed a pin into the opposite corner of the poster. "What's not right about it?"

"It's not old enough."

"It's old enough," Owen muttered resolutely then glanced back to see the concern on the visitor's face. "It came out in the early eighties."

"But you can't sell music past sixty-five."

Owen climbed several steps down the ladder. As he did, he unrolled the poster, covering over the faces of The Big Bopper, Chuck Berry, and Little Richard.

He stuck two pins in the bottom corners of the poster. He then hopped off the ladder and stepped back to ensure his new addition was level.

In the middle of the wall, slightly off-kilter, hung a large image of four long-haired musicians clad in leather and eyeliner. They leered at the viewer with their fists raised in defiance.

The poster clashed with the sensibilities of the store's other memorabilia.

"What is *that*?" the customer said, pointing at the wall.

"That," Owen said, "is Mötley Crüe."

"I know who they are, but you *can't* do that."

He turned to face the naysayer and crossed his arms.

It was then the visitor finally took in the man behind the counter. His gaze traveled up and down the man's massive six-foot-four, two-hundred-twenty-five pound frame.

The customer examined the tattoos on the big man's arms. First, the fireball tattoo on his right hand which turned into a snake encircling his entire arm and disappeared under his shirt. A kaleidoscope of images cascaded down his left.

Owen's outfit consisted of blue jeans and black Converse tennis shoes. His blue T-shirt featured an image of a vinyl record. Its logo read *Rockafellers—Side A—Where the Music Never Dies*.

The smaller man looked up at Owen and swallowed hard. "You're a big fella, aren't you?" The man snickered as he fiddled with a gemstone earring in his left lobe. "You standing on a box back there or something?"

"Why can't I do this?" Owen asked, thumbing toward the Mötley Crüe poster behind him. His gravelly voice lacked any playfulness.

The visitor nervously chuckled. "You can, of course. I didn't mean to tell you what you couldn't do. It's your business, after all. You can do anything you want."

"But you said..."

"I was thinking about your customer base. They're loyal."

"For this dusty stuff?" Owen waved to the boxes of old vinyl records sitting neatly arranged on several rows of folding tables. Underneath the tables were additional cardboard boxes containing more albums.

"For sure. They love it." The visitor didn't sound convincing.

"What about you?" the big man asked. He leaned in slightly. "Are you here to buy something?"

"Well..." the half-naked man glanced around, "not me. No."

Owen smirked and straightened. He shoved his hands in his pockets. "I've been open for two hours, and you're the first person to show up. It doesn't seem like these records are in high demand."

"Just wait until summer, it gets—"

"I don't want to wait 'til then," the big man interrupted. "I want to make a change now. I want to sell what *I* want, what *I* like, which is real rock and roll." Owen lifted his chin toward the speakers. "Heavy metal and hard rock that cranks. Not fuddy-duddy music."

The man rubbed his bare belly and swallowed with some difficulty. When he spoke, his voice was soft, and his words seemed carefully chosen. "Don't get frustrated. It's the off-season. Your store will get downright busy come tourist season. I promise."

"You promise?"

The man stopped mid-rub and glanced to his left and right. "Promise might be too strong of a word."

Owen closed the ladder with a clatter and moved it toward the back of the building. When the big man returned to the front, he found the visitor still staring at the poster. The smaller man absently stroked his braid of hair.

"If you don't like this music," the visitor said, "why did you buy the business?"

Owen considered the question before saying, "I liked the view of the ocean."

"If you change what you sell," the customer said, pointing his braid to the leather-clad musicians, "you're going to compete with Headbangers, and that'll be bad for everybody."

"The store at the end of the boardwalk?"

"They cover everything after sixty-five."

"How come they got all the good stuff?"

The visitor shrugged. "I guess the two stores agreed upon a deal so as not to step on the other's toes. Isn't that how capitalism should be? Working together, hand-in-hand, everybody getting a little, so nobody loses."

Owen's lip curled. "When did this deal get worked out?"

The man released his braid and returned to rubbing his stomach. "You should ask Al, the owner. Maybe you guys can hammer out a new agreement. Maybe he'll give up the rest of the sixties so you could get Jimi and Janis. That would seem fair." A sly smile crossed the visitor's face. "Jimi alone would be worth all of the seventies, am I right?"

His face warmed. "I'm not asking anyone for permission to sell anything. This is my store. I'll sell what I want."

"Relax, man," the visitor said, with a nervous chuckle. His hand suddenly reversed direction on his belly and rubbed counterclockwise. "No need for any machismo. We're rational men here." The visitor's eyes narrowed, and his lips pursed momentarily. When his face relaxed, he pulled his shoulders back and stood a little straighter. "You're the boss."

Owen struggled to comprehend the sudden change in the visitor's demeanor. "I am the boss," he finally said.

"And you've got a head for business."

"I do?"

"It's obvious, which is why there's no more time for trivialities, so to speak."

What is this guy after? Owen wondered.

"Your time is valuable," the visitor continued.

The big man's gaze flitted over the empty store.

"I'm a businessman, too," the visitor said. His hand stopped moving but remained resting on his stomach.

"*You're* a businessman?"

"That's correct," the visitor said, thrusting his hand across the counter. "I'm Sam."

Staring at the sweaty extremity, Owen frowned.

Sam pulled his hand back, examined it quickly, then dried it on his shorts. "The man with a plan."

"Sam," the bigger man muttered, "with a plan."

"Now, you're getting it. And may I ask your name?"

"Hunter."

"*Hunter?*"

Owen's face hardened, and he leaned slightly forward. "Got a problem with that?"

The visitor lifted his hands in mock surrender and nervously chuckled. "No, no, Hunter's a super cool name."

"Thanks."

"For a kid," Sam muttered under his breath.

Owen inhaled deeply before asking, "What exactly are you looking for?"

"It's not what I'm looking for that matters," Sam pointed at Owen, "it's what you're looking for that does."

"Excuse me?"

"Here's the thing," Sam said. "I can get you anything, and I mean *anything*."

Owen's eyes were slitted. "Like what?"

"Name it," the visitor said with a conspiratorial grin.

The big man dismissively waved his hand. He hadn't messed with illicit substances in years, and he had no interest in participating in that type of activity again. "I don't need what you're selling."

"You most certainly do." Sam fiddled with his gemstone earring. "You're new around here. You're gonna need some product, right? Especially if you're looking to make a change." The visitor stepped to a nearby rack of Kingston Trio albums and flipped absently through them. "You'll need to replace all this... What did you call it? Dusty stuff? That's a lot of stock." Sam's fingers continued to flip through albums, but his eyes lifted to scan the store. "You want Def Leppard? I can get them. How about Duran Duran? That's rock and roll for the ladies, am I right? I can find them, too. I can even get Frankie Goes to Hollywood if you like that sort of thing. Or is that not rock and roll enough?"

"You're a scavenger."

Sam spun to him, shocked. "Scavenger? That's hurtful and unnecessary. I mean it. Just plain rude." His hand caressed his long braid of gray hair while he thought. "What if I called you a yard seller? Would you like that?"

Owen scowled.

"Well, no," Sam said with a self-conscious giggle, "you wouldn't. And I wouldn't dare imply such a thing. But you've got me wrong, Hunter. I'm a purveyor of music. Whatever you need, I can get it. For a cost, of course."

"I would expect nothing less."

"There are always people willing to part with their music. If you know who and when to ask."

"Which you do."

"Naturally."

"How do you know these people?"

"I've been in this town since I was a tender young man. I know everybody, so let me help you. It's your first day, right?"

Owen shrugged.

"That's what I thought," Sam said. "We needed to meet before some of the other guys showed up."

"Other guys?"

"There are some shady characters out there who'll try to sell you junk."

"I'm sure."

"But not me," Sam said, proudly thumbing toward his hairless chest. "I'm a legitimate businessman."

"Your attire alone says that."

Sam glanced down to his naked belly, board shorts, and flip-flops. "This is California casual."

"Is that a thing?"

"It's my style. A trademark, if you will. You won't find many like me, Hunter."

Owen smiled. As quirky as the man was, he had a certain charm.

The big man considered the store before returning his attention to the visitor. "Okay, Sam. Bring some stuff around. We'll see what you have and if we can make a deal."

"All right," he said, clapping his hands twice. From the back of his board shorts, Sam pulled out a crumbled and slightly moist business card. He set it on the counter. "That's my number."

The card read *Samuel Peyton—Trader* and listed his phone number.

With the tip of a pencil, Owen slid the card behind a porcelain statue of a young Elvis Presley. Frozen in a permanent sway with arms thrust out, the king of rock and roll stood in front of a microphone.

The visitor stepped back to leave. "Call me any—"

A large orange cat wandered out from under a display rack and stared at Sam. With a widening smile, he asked, "You have a cat?"

"You want him?"

Sam reached down and gently stroked the tom's head. "What's its name?"

"It's your choice."

"That's weird. Is it Turkish or something? Lakota, maybe?"

Owen opened his mouth but quickly closed it. Instead, he watched the visitor pet the cat.

When the man stood, he said, "See you around, Yerchoise."

To Owen, he said, "I'll be back with some goods. You won't be sorry."

The sweaty, rotund man then hurried to the front of the store and opened the door, which let in the ocean's aroma.

He faced the big man once more.

"Welcome to Costa Buena, my friend." With an extravagant wave, he said, "May the community be good to you."

Chapter 2

Shortly after noon, the door to the store swung open again, and a red-haired woman marched in. She wore a pleated print skirt and a double-breasted jacket. In her left hand, she clutched a wooden clipboard to her chest.

Her eyes didn't linger over the store. Instead, they immediately focused on Owen as he stood behind the counter. He was in the process of listing things he'd like to update in the business.

The woman stomped over. "Are you the new owner?"

"Excuse me?"

Her eyes focused on the dancing Elvis statue. For a moment, she stared at it. When she glanced up, her attention diverted to the newest poster behind the counter. Her lips twisted in disapproval.

"What?" Owen said.

She refocused on him. "The owner? Is that you?"

"Yeah, I'm—"

"Anita Moffett," she said and stabbed a business card toward him.

Owen reluctantly took the card but didn't read it. His eyes held hers, waiting for an explanation as to why she was there.

Anita, on the other hand, repeatedly flicked her gaze downward.

Finally, Owen's eyes dropped and read the business card.

Anita Moffett, Director
Costa Buena's Business Welcoming
and Standards Committee.

"That's a mouthful," he said, setting the card next to Samuel Peyton's.

"And your name?" she asked.

"Hunter."

"And last?"

He paused before saying with a slight shake of his head, "Hunter."

She deftly lifted her clipboard and readied her pen with a click of its end cap. "Your name is Hunter Hunter?"

"No, it's—"

"Says here," she muttered, "that your name is Owen Hunter."

"I should have said it's Owen."

"Hunter Owen?"

"That's what I wanted, but—"

"These people," Anita murmured. "They never get anything right." She lined through his name and wrote *Hunter Owen*. When she looked up, she said, "We've been alerted that an application was filed notifying the city about a change in ownership."

"And?"

"When did this transfer take place?"

"Today's my first day."

She rolled her eyebrows, sighed heavily, then tapped her clipboard. "It's highly unlikely you purchased the business today."

"No, I guess not."

"When did this occur?"

He shrugged. "A week ago, probably."

"*Probably?* You don't know the exact date?"

"Not off the top of my head."

Anita's face reddened. "How can you not know? This is *your* business, isn't it?"

"Yes," Owen said, now irritated by the woman's presence. "But I'm not usually focused on that type of stuff."

She harrumphed. "Not focused? You should be. It's your business. I'll put in today's date as a placeholder, but you really should know that kind of thing."

"If you have a copy of the application, wouldn't the date of transfer be listed?"

Her eyes narrowed. "That information—"

Something fell in the rear of the store, and Anita's head jerked toward the sound.

"What was that?" she asked.

"The cat."

Her jaw dropped. "You're blaming a cat? What kind of person—"

"He knocks stuff off the counters and shelves all the time. He's neurotic that way."

Anita's eyes widened. "Cats are *not* neurotic. They are gentle creatures."

"Not this one."

As if summoned, the orange tom appeared.

"Who's this good boy?" she asked in a suddenly sweet voice as the cat rubbed against her legs. The pinched nature of her face relaxed.

It may have been the first time Owen was happy to see the feline.

"He seems perfectly wonderful to me," Anita said.

"That's because you don't know him. He's a monster."

"Shh," she hissed and bent over to pet the cat. "Don't call him that. He's a good boy, aren't you?"

"You can have him."

"I already have four," she said, her voice rising in pitch as if talking to a child. She stroked the tom from head to tail. "If I were to bring you into our home, it would upset our delicate ecosystem. Wouldn't it?"

Owen watched her with growing disdain. A woman with four cats was worse than a woman with four children. At least the children would eventually grow and leave the house. The cats would be with her forever.

Four cats, the big man mused, would run her life. They would overwhelm her thoughts. She seemed the type to name them things like Mister Whiskerbottoms or Annabelle Fuzzyfeet.

His upper lip curled as he imagined furniture covered with cat hair, little fur-covered toys strewn about her house, and a cat calendar hanging in her kitchen.

The woman cooed to the tom. "You're a handsome boy, aren't you? The handsomest boy in the whole store."

Owen bristled at that comment. He was far more handsome than the scruffy tom.

As Anita straightened, Owen wiped his face clean of any emotion.

"What's his name?" she asked, still smiling at the cat.

"You can choose."

Her smile morphed into a scowl, and she slowly turned to the big man. "Excuse me? He doesn't have a name?"

Owen leaned on the counter and became very serious. With her affection for cats, he knew she would appreciate what he was about to share. "You can choose its name. You see, cats are a reflection of the person they are with at any given time. Therefore, that person should be able to name them. Pretty cool, huh?"

The woman stared at him, processing his words. Her knuckles whitened as she gripped the clipboard tighter. "That—"

"Oh, I almost forgot," Owen said. "The only condition to the naming rule is it must be a musician. It is a record store cat, after all. Can't have you name it after a movie star or a cartoon character."

As the big man's grin widened, Anita's face reddened.

"That—" she stammered, "that is absolutely the *most* disrespectful thing I have ever heard."

His grin faded since he hadn't expected that reaction. He thought she would appreciate the naming rule. Up until now, everyone else had.

"A cat is a person," Anita said.

"A person?"

"With a soul."

"A person with a soul?"

She shook her head, struggling to hold back her anger. "Renaming them on a whim is hurtful and demeaning. I have a good mind to report you to animal control."

Owen's chin fell to his chest.

"You, sir, are the monster. Not this sweet boy." She bent to pet the tom once more. "Aren't you a good boy, Paul McCatney?"

The big man recoiled. "You can't do that," he said.

"What?" she said.

"No cute names."

She continued to stroke the cat from head to tail. "Who said?"

"I did."

Anita stood, crossed her arms, and jerked her head to the side. "That wasn't part of your rules."

"Yes, it was. I just forgot to tell you."

Her stare hardened. "Really?"

"Really. You have to change his name."

Her eyes flicked to the cat then back to Owen. "David Meowie."

Owen threw his arms into the air. "No! No cute cat names. Not in my store."

"I'm abiding by your rules, Mr. Owen. You're the one changing the rules when you don't like the outcome."

He waved a finger. "No," he said, unsure why he was so upset about a silly cat name. But he couldn't stop himself. "You either name it after a musician, or you don't get to name it at all."

"Fine," Anita said with a shrug.

"*Fine.*"

The woman stared at the tom for several moments. Finally, she turned to the big man with a malicious grin.

"It better not be cute," Owen said, his voice low and menacing.

"Cat Stevens."

The big man sighed.

She bent over and rubbed the tom behind the ear. "Who's a smart boy, Cat Stevens? The smartest boy in the whole store."

The big man's frustration level now boiled. "Why are you here?"

"I am here to discuss your intentions for this business."

"My intentions?"

Anita straightened and forcefully nodded. "Yes, sir, your intentions. We want to know what you're planning to do with your business. And, if how you treat your cat is any indication of how you plan to treat the community, we're going to have some serious problems."

"I plan to sell records," Owen said, "same as the previous owner. Hopefully, make some money. Is that okay?"

Anita clicked her tongue.

"I suppose that's the wrong answer."

She stared at him as if he were simple. "Here in Costa Buena, we are looking for a better—"

"Class?" Owen interrupted.

Shocked, the woman pulled back. "No, sir! We would never say that. We do not discriminate against anyone."

"I apologize. I thought—"

"We simply want a better type of business owner."

Owen frowned. "I don't understand."

"We want business operators who add to the community thread rather than pull from it."

"It sounds like you want businesses that aren't interested in making money."

"Exactly," she said.

"But if they don't make money—"

"Tsk. Spoken like a capitalist." She ticked something on her clipboard. "I should have known."

It was the first time he'd ever been accused of being a capitalist, and Owen wasn't sure he liked it. He reread her business card. "And you're with the local government?"

Anita pointed her pen at Owen. "I'm with the people."

"Is that the government?"

"I'm with the *people*, and we expect a standard to be maintained in our community. Do you understand?"

"Not really, no."

She reached into her purse, pulled out a pamphlet, and thrust it toward him. When he didn't take it, she slapped it onto the counter. "This will tell you everything you need to know."

He unfolded the colorful brochure, which was titled *Understanding Your Responsibilities and Duties as a Business Owner in Costa Buena.*

"Read it," she said, "learn it, live it."

Owen's gaze glossed over the various things for which he should be responsible as a member of the business community.

She inhaled deeply, closed her eyes for a moment, then exhaled. When Anita opened her eyes, she said, "Welcome to Costa Buena, Mr. Owen." Then she pointed at him and furrowed her brow. "You *better* be good for this community."

Chapter 3

"Costa Buena is a fantastic community," U.S. Marshal Theodore 'Ted' Onderdonk said. "You're gonna love it."

Beauregard Smith shifted in the booth. "You said that about the last community, and it almost got me killed."

"Costa Buena is different. I promise."

They were seated at Marty's Big Boy, a family-style restaurant in Provo, Utah.

Beau had been on the run for two weeks before he called Onderdonk. He could have pushed it further, but he was dangerously low on cash and didn't have any credit cards. He couldn't apply for one under his real name nor the fake one the Marshal Service had given him previously while he resided in Pleasant Valley, Maine.

Besides, crisscrossing middle America on his chopper was bound to end badly with both the Satan's Dawgs Motorcycle Club (MC) and the east coast mafia chasing after him.

He knew he would have to stop sooner or later. When he crossed into Utah from Wyoming, he figured it was time. Beau rented a storage unit under a false name with the last of his cash and parked his motorcycle inside. He paid a year in advance and was now completely broke.

The big man considered the marshal. When he walked in, he noticed the marshal's outfit was the same as he always wore—short-sleeve plaid shirt, khaki pants, and loafers. On his hip were his badge and gun. Sitting before him was a stack of pancakes with heavy butter. Instead of syrup, he smeared marmalade over the top and in between the layers.

"Costa Buena?" Beau asked. "Where's that?"

"In California," Onderdonk said, stuffing a bite into his mouth. "A bit south of San Francisco. A little north of San Diego."

"That's helpful."

"Don't be a whiner, Beau. You'll find it."

His eyes slanted. Only Onderdonk could get away with talking to him like that. He was a little more careful with how he did it now after the incident in Maine, but the marshal still had that mischievous glint in his eye. Beau respected Onderdonk's lack of fear when engaging with him in banter.

"We've got another business for you to run," the marshal said around a mouthful of food.

"Another business? What happened to the old owner?"

"He died," Onderdonk said, cutting another hunk of pancake. "Naturally."

Beau tilted his head.

"He drowned."

His eyes widened. "Drowning is natural?"

"Don't be so sensitive." The marshal shoved another forkful into his mouth. As he chewed, he said, "The guy was in his mid-eighties. He'd go for a daily swim out in the ocean. One day, the tide was too much for him. Local cops ruled it an accidental death."

"Sounds like a horrible way to go."

"Any way you go is horrible."

Beau pushed his scrambled eggs around his plate.

"But he lived a happy life for almost forty years while in our protection. No one ever found him. Now, we'll slide you into the business. Easy peasy."

"Easy peasy."

"Trust me."

"The last time I did that—"

"I didn't mean for any of that to happen."

"But it did. I almost got killed, and I left behind a girl I really liked and—"

"I know, Beau. I know. I am sorry about that."

The two men ate silently for a bit.

The lawman had placed Beau into a U.S. Marshal-owned business after another of their witnesses had gone missing. The proverbial worm on a hook, Beau soon got sideways with a well-connected mobster. When things turned deadly, he ran. Now, instead of just the MC wanting him dead, the east coast mob wanted his head as well.

Beau set down his fork. "Did you get in trouble?"

"For what?"

"Seriously, did you get in trouble?"

"I found a missing witness."

"That was me," Beau said, thumping his chest. "I did that. *I* found her."

"But I planned to stick you into her previous location. That took initiative."

The big man glanced around the restaurant then leaned in. He lowered his voice but added emphasis to it. "You burned two covers and a business that was a marshal asset. What did the agency do, Ted? Did they slap your hand? Come on."

The marshal took a break from his stack of pancakes as the melted butter congealed on his plate. He lifted his coffee mug in mock salute. "They didn't slap my hand."

"They give you a medal?"

"Not a medal, no."

"A raise? Tell me they didn't give you a raise."

"I'm a government employee, Beau. They don't hand out raises willy-nilly."

"Why won't you tell me?

The lawman shrugged. "It was nothing. Just a letter of commendation."

Silence fell over the table. Beau shook his head, lifted his fork, and jammed some eggs into his mouth.

The news about Onderdonk's commendation didn't lessen Beau's appetite. He wasn't the type of man to let something like that upset him. He knew how to handle anger and hatred. Although he wasn't angry at the moment, and he didn't hate the marshal. He was convinced now more than ever that the government was a game rigged against ordinary people. To him, this was an undeniable truth, and Beau didn't shy away from such things.

When he finished eating, the big man pushed his empty plate away. "So this business, what is it?"

"It's a record store."

Beau slowly smiled. "A record store?"

"Yeah."

"On the California coast? Maybe it won't be so bad. What kind of record store?"

"Oldies. Fifties and sixties type of stuff."

Beau's face scrunched. "Like Elvis Presley and Buddy Holly? Do I look like the type of guy who listens to that?"

The lawman shrugged. "Change it to the stuff you like. I don't care."

"Really?"

"For sure. It's going to be your store, Beau. Do what you want. Besides, it's California. They probably listen to that same screechy stuff you do."

He smirked.

Onderdonk chuckled for a moment before saying, "Listen. I'm trying to make it up to you. This is one of our best gigs. It's a sweet deal. For real. We've even got a little house around the way, a block from the beach. It's not much, but you can swim in the morning, work a couple of hours, close down for lunch and grab some sun, work a couple more hours, then close out the day on the beach. What more could you ask for?"

"Not to drown in the ocean."

"He was in his eighties."

"We're in the fall now," Beau said flatly.

"And it'll be summer again in a few months. That's how a calendar works."

"Whatever."

"I could have sent you to a dairy farm in Duluth."

"You wouldn't dare."

"The Dawgs would never chase you there. It being Minnesota and all."

Beauregard Smith sighed. Once the feared bookkeeper for the Satan's Dawgs Motorcycle Club, he'd been forced to turn informant for the FBI. Immediately upon doing so, he'd become Public Enemy Number One for the MC, and their highest priority was to hunt him down.

In the Dawgs, positions of power were given coded titles. This was to make their activities sound legitimate in the event the FBI or another law enforcement agency tapped their phones or recorded their conversations.

As the club's bookkeeper, Beau 'kept book' on those who crossed the club. He then 'cleared the books' whenever necessary. A long line of dead men lay in his wake. It was this skill and experience that had kept Beau alive so far.

"If you slide back under our umbrella," the marshal said, "it'll be the same rules as before."

"I understand," the big man said and sipped from his coffee.

Do not contact people from your old life.
Do not visit places from your old life.
Do not develop habits from your old life.

They were simple rules, and he tried to abide by them at his last stop, but that was a small town in Maine. There weren't many opportunities to get in trouble, and yet he still managed to run afoul of the mob. The new location in California might pose additional problems. He imagined there could be a lot of opportunities that could trip him up.

He shook the worries away and asked, "What's Ekleberry up to?"

Federal Agent Maxwell Ekleberry had discovered the one thing Beau loved more than the motorcycle club—his grandmother—and used it to turn him into an informant. In reality, Beau already had one foot out the door when it came to the Satan's Dawgs, but he never imagined himself getting into bed with the federal government.

"Haven't talked with him much since the incident in Pleasant Valley."

"He wasn't happy with what you did?"

Onderdonk nodded. "I've got some making up to do. Same thing I'm trying to do with you."

"And you're sending me to Costa Buena as a way of apology?"

"Unless you want that gig in Minnesota. I hear it's nice in the winter."

Beau rolled his eyes. "California, here I come."

"We should probably talk about your new name."

"I can't be Brody Steele any longer?"

"Are you serious? Have you checked the website lately?"

The mob owned a secret website—www.thefbiisabunchofdirtyrats.com—which kept track of all the informants known to be in the Witness Protection Program.

The Marshal Service learned of the website from a mob analyst turned informant. Onderdonk revealed this information to Beau while they were in Maine. The marshals had a hacker in their program that set them up with backdoor access to the website. This allowed the law enforcement community to spy on the mob while they tried to track their missing informants. Knowing the criminal underground was that organized surprised Beau. He'd never heard of the website while he was in the Dawgs. He never even imagined such a thing could exist.

On the website, every known-to-be-living mob informant was listed. Even though he wasn't associated with the mob, Beau's photo and profile appeared on their site. Somehow, the Dawgs had gotten him included. Or perhaps the mafia tracked anyone affiliated with the Witness Security Program. He wasn't sure how he ended up on the website, but it spooked him. One day, he'd like to know how he ended up there.

The site displayed his real name, his physical attributes, and the various tattoos he had. It also had computer-manipulated photographs showing what he might look like with different haircuts, hair colors, facial hair, glasses, and hats.

"They know Brody Steele now," Onderdonk said. "It's listed as an alias under your real name. You already know the cover was burned in Maine. That means it's burned everywhere. There's no going back, so remove it from your head. Don't even think about it."

It made sense, but it was another slap of his new reality. He wasn't even three months out of prison, and he'd been relocated, exposed by the mob, and forced to run. He'd crossed the entire country so far managing to hide from his former crew.

At least, he was about to get another identity and another chance at becoming a better man.

Turning rat was harder than he expected.

"What's my new name?"

"Owen."

"Owen?" Beau said. "That's a nerd name."

Onderdonk handed him a file with a driver's license clipped to the outside cover.

"Owen Hunter?" the big man said, reading the California identification card. "Why can't it be Hunter Owen? Hunter is way cooler."

"You don't need cool, Beau. You need boring. It's better this way. Remember, you need to keep a low profile. That's what the WitSec program is all about. Keeping you safe. We're only able to do that when you maintain a low profile."

Beau's lip curled as he read the name. "Owen Hunter. Ugh. Will you consult me next time?"

The lawman leaned in. "There better not be a next time. I've done this twice for you now, which is once more than I do for most people in the program."

"That wasn't my fault."

Onderdonk leaned back and picked up his coffee mug. "I know it wasn't. It was my fault, and I'll own that. That's why I'm trying to make it up to you."

Beau stared at the new driver's license. "But Owen? Really?" he said. He hated the new name.

"You're going to do fine," Onderdonk said. "Trust me. This is like riding a bike. You fell off—"

"I didn't fall off. I was pushed."

"You've got to get back on that bike and start pedaling."

"As *Owen.*"

"Stop whining, Beau. This is going to work out great. You're going to love California."

Beau had to admit he had liked California whenever the Dawgs rode through the Golden State.

The lawman rapped his knuckles on the edge of the table. "I've also got a surprise for you."

Looking up from the license he held in his hands, Beau said, "I don't like surprises. You know that."

"Wait until you see it," U.S. Marshal Ted Onderdonk said with a gleeful smile. "You're gonna love it."

Chapter 4

The orange cat stared at him from the middle of the shop. He paused midlick with his tongue stuck to its paw. He was the surprise Onderdonk referenced. It was the one thing Owen had been happy to leave behind in Pleasant Valley, Maine.

"I don't like you," the big man said.

Unimpressed by his disdain, the cat dragged its tongue across its paw.

Owen turned his attention to his computer, and the website he'd just called up—www.thefbiisabunchofdirtyrats.com.

A simple screen with two fields—Username and Password—filled the monitor.

He entered *Guest* and *Password* into the appropriate places. These unimaginative entries were created by a hacker squirreled away somewhere in the U.S. Marshal's program. At least, Owen wouldn't forget them.

Once he was into the system, he could see any living person the mob and their affiliates currently expected to be hiding under the umbrella of the Witness Protection Program. He scrolled through the list of informants until he found his real name—Beauregard Smith. When he clicked his photograph, he was taken to a new screen.

Several computer-manipulated photos showed him with different hairstyles and facial hair. The site also detailed his tattoos with pictures of each. Somehow, they'd gotten these from his separate prison stays and his jail booking photos.

There were also pictures of him that had been cropped out of Satan's Dawg functions. They showed him walking, standing, and smiling.

The site listed his aliases. So far, there was only one—Brody Steele.

It also displayed a list of sightings. Pleasant Valley, Maine, was the only location where anyone had seen him.

On the screen, his current location read *UNKNOWN*.

At the bottom of the screen was a bright blue button that read *Click for Real-Time Updates.*

The big man rubbed the side of his face. The list of sightings, location status, and real-time updates were new developments. As of a couple of weeks ago, these had not existed.

Whoever maintained this website for the mob and its associates were providing them with upgrades. The locations, both last seen and current, didn't bother him as much as those five words—*Click for Real-Time Updates.*

"This isn't good," Owen said to the empty store.

If someone signed up for these updates, the moment someone saw his location, they could notify the webmaster—was there an alert process he didn't know about?—and anyone hunting would immediately be directed toward him. Owen imagined all the Dawgs now being signed up for this alert. Would the east coast mafia be signed up for this as well? He assumed so. That meant a lot of bad men would come running toward him if the system ever sent an alert.

Looking up, he saw the tom continue cleaning himself, completely unconcerned. "This affects you, too, you know?"

Owen wanted to click the update button and see what kind of information they requested. Maybe they wanted a cell phone number where they could text info. Perhaps an email address where an alert could be sent. But most guys only had cell numbers. He had never had an email. Who would he send an email to?

Using the computer mouse, he maneuvered the cursor over the words. His finger hovered over the mouse button, wanting to click it to get the real-time updates on himself.

However, if he did that, was he providing them with a way to track him? He knew the government and the police could track a person through cell phones, which is why he only used burner phones whenever he needed one. Right now, he refused to use one and would only use the old landline that came with the store.

Owen slid the cursor away. His fears about tracking through cell phones led him to wonder if the mob could follow him back to Costa Buena because he visited this website. Was that even possible? The big man had only the most basic understanding of technology, but maybe they could. A cold sweat formed at the base of his back.

If they could track him to the coast of California, what stopped them from following his digital breadcrumbs to this exact building?

He hurriedly closed the browser and stared at the empty screen.

The door to the store opened, allowing in the chilly Pacific breeze.

A man in his late twenties with short hair and a carefully manicured five o'clock shadow sauntered in. He wore a white short-sleeved shirt, skinny black jeans, and black loafers. A pair of black-framed glasses perched on his nose.

Stepping into the middle of the store, he spun toward Owen and quickly said, "Got any Kinks?"

"That's a little personal."

The cat froze, its tongue protruding and paw extended. It cautiously watched the younger man.

"What I meant was—" He stopped and tilted his head, listening to the music playing from the hanging speakers.

The orange tom returned to cleaning itself.

The visitor's nose crinkled, and confusion flooded his eyes. He pointed toward a speaker. "That isn't the right era."

"Said the man dressed like a reject from *Ozzie and Harriet.*" Owen remembered watching the old television show while spending summers with his grandmother.

The hipster pushed his glasses up his nose.

"So, what are you looking for?" Owen asked.

"Kinks," the visitor said.

"We're not that kind of store."

The hipster's face clouded. "*The* Kinks. 'All Day and All of the Night.' Not ringing a bell? Come on, man, you must have heard of them. You own a record store."

"Of course, I've heard of them," Owen said. "They had that other big hit."

"'Lola.'"

"That's the one," he said with a snap of his fingers. He had no idea what the nerd was talking about. "They'll be over there somewhere." He pointed toward various boxes of records.

The hipster wandered among the various racks of vinyl albums.

Another breeze entered the store as the door reopened. The new visitor was in his mid-fifties, about twenty years older than Owen and about the same size. His outfit consisted of jeans and black Converse and a blue T-shirt that read *Headbangers—Where Rock Still Rolls*. Tattoos of guitars and musical symbols ran up and down his exposed arms.

Owen glanced down at his clothing. He and the visitor could have dressed from the same closet.

The man's face pinched as he looked at the speakers hanging in the corner of the ceiling. He shook his head, then strode to the counter. The cat bolted under a display rack.

"You can't do that," he announced and pointed into the air.

"Do what?" Owen asked.

"That!" he said, stabbing a finger toward a speaker. "That music belongs in my store."

"You don't own the airwaves," Owen said. "It's the radio."

When the visitor noticed the Mötley Crüe poster, his face darkened. "And that!"

Owen glanced back at the poster and smiled. "Cool, huh?"

"I own that decade. That was the deal."

"Not with me."

The visitor glared at him. "Prescott cut the deal."

"Prescott?"

"Prescott Honeywell," the visitor said, thumping a finger on the counter. "He owned this dump before you."

"Dump?"

"How do you not know his name?"

Owen shrugged.

"You bought the business from his estate, didn't you?"

"My attorney did the paperwork."

Usually, mentioning an attorney in situations like this was a useful way to end most conversations.

"*Your* attorney?" the visitor said. "You want to bring attorneys into this? How about I call my attorney, tough guy? I've got one, too."

Owen hadn't expected that reaction.

"I had a verbal contract with the previous owner of this business which you bought. I believe the contract and its responsibilities passed to you." The man pointed his finger vigorously at Owen while he spoke. "You are bound by the terms of that agreement."

In his previous life as a Satan's Dawg, Owen would have ended the conversation right then. A well-placed punch to the throat took the fight out of most men.

But he couldn't do that. He couldn't risk exposing himself, not only to the local authorities but to the citizens living in the community. He needed to keep a low profile, as Onderdonk had said. Therefore, he had to fight his battles the way most people did—verbally.

That didn't mean he had to do it like a wimp, though. Owen stepped from around the counter to stand nose to nose with his accuser. It wasn't often he faced off with men his size. The visitor wasn't intimidated.

"Who said I couldn't sell this music?"

"I did!" the visitor said, his nose almost touching Owen's.

He lowered his voice. "Not going to happen, old man."

Offended, the visitor stepped back. "Old man?"

"I can sell whatever I want."

"No," the visitor said, shaking his head. "You can't. Prescott and I had an agreement."

"Your agreement is anti-American."

"No, it isn't."

"It was anti-competition and anti-American."

The visitor's face pinched. "I believe in America."

Owen leaned in and asked conspiratorially, "Are you a communist?"

"What? No!"

"Well, that's good, because I'm bringing competition to your doorstep. God bless the USA." Owen saluted the visitor.

"You can't!"

"It's done. Seventies, eighties, and nineties. All of it. I'm gonna start selling it."

"You can't!" the visitor repeated. "Those are mine. The agreement—"

"What about it?" Owen shrugged.

"Three decades!" the visitor yelled, holding up as many fingers. "Prescott didn't want anything newer than sixty-five. He got the better part of the deal when we started."

"Says you. Got this agreement in writing somewhere?"

The visitor's face reddened.

"If it's not in writing, then it doesn't exist."

The man took another half-step back, his eyes running Owen's length. "Who do you think you are?"

"I'm the guy bringing old-fashioned competition to this environmentally friendly town." A smirk crossed Owen's face. "You're welcome."

He should have expected it, but he'd allowed overconfidence to creep in. The punch whipped out, catching him on the chin. It was quicker and harder than expected.

Owen collapsed into a display of discount records.

The visitor stood over him. "There's more where that came from, sunshine. Don't forget it." He then turned and strolled from the store.

As Owen slowly returned to his feet, the display of records crumbled around him. Now upright, he rubbed his jaw, and his eyes burned with rage. He promised himself he'd never get sucker-punched by that guy again.

"I owe you one," he muttered.

It slowly occurred to him that someone had stood by watching the whole interaction. He slowly turned to see the hipster, now holding a Kinks record tightly to his chest.

The younger man smiled awkwardly. "Big Al is pretty protective of his store."

"Big Al?"

"Al Ferguson."

"What's he got to be protective of? It's a record store like this one, right?"

The hipster glanced around. "His is nicer and cleaner." When he returned his attention to Owen, he noticed the big man's scowl. "But basically, the same. Like you said."

"So, what's he need to be protective of?"

The hipster leaned in and glanced around before speaking. "I don't know, but I think he's got something going on down there."

"Like what?"

"I haven't been able to figure it out. Occasionally, he kicks some of us out of the store for no reason just to close up shop for an hour or so."

"What's he say he's doing?"

The younger man shrugged. "Says he has to do some stocking or something lame like that. He pulls the shades, and a little later reopens.

He's sort of odd that way, and that's saying something for this town."

"When he reopens, does it look like he's restocked?"

"I never think so."

Owen studied the hipster who soon glanced at the album he held in his hands.

"But I haven't looked too closely to tell you the truth. Maybe he has."

The big man moved his jaw around. Al threw a pretty good punch for a guy in his fifties.

The young man glanced at the broken display before asking, "Can I pay for this now?"

The two moved toward the counter. Owen checked the price of the album, rang it up on the register, and announced it.

The younger man removed a carefully folded wad of cash and pulled off several small bills. "What brought you to Costa Buena?" the hipster asked.

Taking the money from the hipster, Owen said, "The weather."

"Seems like you're new to the industry."

"How could you tell?"

"It's obvious. What did you do before?"

"I was a bookkeeper."

"Were you good at your job?"

"I was the best."

The visitor's eyes narrowed. "Then, why do this? Doesn't seem as stable."

Owen handed him his change. "You ask a lot of questions."

"I'm naturally inquisitive, I guess."

"What do you do?"

The young man smiled. "I'm a manager."

"What do you manage?"

Glancing at the album, *Kinksize Session,* he said, "People and situations."

"Well, that's cryptic."

The hipster raised the album, smiled, and said, "Have a nice day."

He walked out without looking back.

Chapter 5

He finished the day with a few visitors.

First, an out-of-town couple came late in the afternoon. They were on the hunt for early records by The Beach Boys and were excited to find a couple of 45s. While they browsed, though, the husband repeatedly complained of the new style of music playing through the store's stereo.

"It's like a chainsaw cutting concrete," he said,

Owen thought that funny because Concrete Chainsaw seemed like an excellent name for a heavy metal band.

Before taking over the store, he'd gotten a quick lesson from the U.S. Marshals on how to run a cash register, track inventory, and report sales. When he took over the bookstore in Pleasant Valley, he'd ignored the marshals' lessons, thinking himself above it all. His lack of knowledge quickly backfired. To many bookstore customers, he didn't act the part. Therefore, he immediately outed himself as someone not befitting a business owner. This time he paid close attention to what the agents said, and he took notes.

Now, in Costa Buena, he had an opportunity to remake Rockafellers in his image. Since the government bankrolled the venture, making a profit wasn't necessary. However, he could at least attempt to operate in a fashion that would make him proud.

It was another step in the reinvention of himself.

He no longer wanted to be Beauregard Smith, the former bookkeeper for the Satan's Dawgs. He wanted to be a decent man who lived a normal life among ordinary citizens. While in Maine, he learned people actually talked with him if he didn't look intimidating. He found he enjoyed the simple act of smiling at other human beings and having them smile back.

With jeans and a T-shirt, he didn't look as stuffy as he did in Pleasant Valley. His new wardrobe was appropriate for a used record store, and he felt more like himself dressed this way. Khakis and plaid shirts weren't his style.

He thought California was going to be a great fit for him. He'd have to thank Onderdonk for the relocation. Showing gratitude would also be another step toward his reinvention.

The second visitor to enter the store did so with a skateboard tucked under his arm. He wore a sleeveless army jacket, a ripped T-shirt, cut-off jean shorts, and black combat boots. He was in his late twenties, and his bald head glistened under the overhead lights. His nose and lip were pierced multiple times, and his T-shirt read *Punk's Not Dead*.

The new visitor didn't bother looking around. Instead, he immediately approached the counter. He pressed his lips tightly together and breathed loudly through his nose.

Owen forced a polite smile and asked, "Can I help you?"

"You the new owner?" His words quickly tumbled out.

Anytime someone started a conversation with those words, the resulting conversation never went well. Owen's smile faded. "That's right."

Excitement flared in the punk's eyes. "Lucky for you. I'm the welcoming committee."

"A committee of one?"

"I misspoke," he said, curling his lip which exposed a missing tooth in the upper-left corner of his mouth. "I meant to say I'm the *un*welcoming committee."

Owen's smile returned. "You're using committee wrong."

The punk blinked a couple of times. "What?"

"Committee is for two or more people. You should probably say you're a messenger."

"I'm not a messenger for nobody."

Owen shrugged, "Which means you're a messenger for somebody."

The punk blinked several times before asking, "What?"

"You used a double negative."

"A double what?"

"Who sent you?"

The punk's face tightened. "No one sent me," he said defensively. "I sent myself."

"Led by the best, no doubt."

"What?"

Owen crossed his arms and watched the younger man.

The visitor started to say something, but the orange cat stepped out from underneath a nearby display and diverted his attention. He glared at the tom. "I hate cats."

"He's not so fond of you, either."

"Pfft," the punk said, "Go. Get."

The cat didn't move.

"He doesn't listen to people he doesn't know," Owen said. "Stranger danger and all."

The punk turned to Owen. "What?"

"You're doing well," he said. "Keep going."

"What?"

"Why don't you tell me what you want?"

The man's face reddened before blurting, "You need to pay."

"What am I paying for?"

"For protection."

The punk jerked his head and shoulders forward in what was supposed to be an intimidating manner. Owen wasn't impressed.

"Protection?" he asked.

"That's right."

"From who?"

The younger man blinked several times before saying, "Things can get dangerous around here."

Owen walked around the counter to stand in front of the visitor. He stood half a foot taller than the punk. "Let me get this straight. You," he tapped the smaller man on the chest before pointing to himself, "are threatening me?"

The punk swallowed with some difficulty. "Uh... no."

"No?"

"No... *sir?*"

"If you're not threatening me, then what are you doing?"

"Collecting."

"I'm not paying for protection I don't need."

"That's not a good idea," the punk muttered.

Owen shrugged. "I'm full of not-so-good ideas. That's what brought me here."

The smaller man took several steps back. He lifted his skateboard in a threatening manner.

"What are you going to do with that?" the big man asked.

The punk's eyes darted about it. Finally, he swung the skateboard, hitting the dancing Elvis Presley statue on the counter. It exploded into dozens of pieces, spreading them across the store.

The cat screeched and sprinted away, disappearing under a nearby display rack.

"Now, you'll take me serious!" the visitor yelled. "You better pay or—"

Stepping quickly forward, Owen slapped the punk hard across the face. The smaller man dropped his skateboard and collapsed to the ground. The big man then lifted the visitor by the back of his jacket and dragged him to the door.

Owen opened it and shoved the extortionist outside.

The punk spun around and said, "My skateboard—"

"Is mine now. Consider it payment for the statue you broke."

"But—"

"You break it; you buy it."

"But—"

"Don't come back."

The punk stood on the boardwalk, rubbing his cheek and staring at Owen. He struggled for his next words. Not finding any, he said, "But—"

The big man stepped outside the store.

The punk turned and sprinted away.

Chapter 6

After cleaning up the broken Elvis statue—he never could locate its head—Owen prepared to close the store. It wasn't even five, but the lack of customers and the confrontation with the punk had put him into a foul mood.

He attempted to open the two sets of roller shades over the front windows. The sun was setting in the west, and Rockafellers was bright and uncomfortably warm. He could see some of the albums near the window were already sun-bleached.

The first set of window shades was stuck. As he tugged repeatedly, he grew increasingly frustrated. He stared up at the rolled set and wondered what he was doing wrong. Concluding he was doing everything correctly, Owen reached up with both hands and yanked. The shade pulled free from the window casing and noisily crashed to the floor.

"Great," he muttered.

He stepped to the next roll of shades, grasped the edge, and tugged firmly. There was no resistance this time, and it opened quickly. Unfortunately, there was no shade provided. The middle of the blind was missing. It appeared its interior had become brittle over the years and crumbled from the inside. Only the stitched edging remained. He tugged on the bottom, and the center-less shade rolled up, loudly clattering as it did.

After collecting the remains of the fallen first set of shades, he walked to the rear of the store, opened the door to the alley, and shoved them into the trash can. He'd deal with the shade issue another time. He then collected the trash from under the counter and threw that away, too.

While in the back, he considered the alley. It was in his nature to always contemplate an escape route. The alley ran parallel to the boardwalk. On the opposite side were houses fronting Main Street, their backyard fences running the entire length. Weeds and trash were everywhere, and ruts lined the center of the unpaved alley. It was a dirty and depressing access point—nothing like the lively, fun boardwalk out front.

He shut the back door and secured it.

Owen then locked the store and walked along the coast.

As far as boardwalks go, it was short, about the length of three city blocks. However, the city had white sandy beaches and a protective shoreline, which made it a destination for tourists and day-trippers wanting a pleasant getaway.

Multi-colored buildings of varying heights and textures decorated the short stretch of development. Commerce took place on one side while on its opposite was the vastness of the ocean. Behind the boardwalk, the city of Costa Buena buffered it before the Pacific Coast Highway ran by. It was a quaint hideaway from the hustle and bustle of most California activity.

Marshal Onderdonk told him the area was built before the skyrocketing cost of housing. He imagined the boardwalk would be worth more torn down and rebuilt as luxury homes or condominiums, but the community had banded together in the early seventies and filed ordinances to protect any redevelopment to the boardwalk. Costa Buena took great pride in its eclectic and colorful nature.

Seeing how Anita Moffett defended the boardwalk, he could only imagine the difficulty in getting things done within the city. It was no wonder why things looked as if everything was frozen in time—stuck in the late sixties.

Near the southern end of the boardwalk, a pier jutted into the ocean. At its furthest end stood a giant Ferris wheel known as El Gato Grande. Several small stands lined the dock, selling refreshments, churros, and frozen bananas. A line of people stood along the wooden railing with fishing lines dropped into the water.

Owen admitted it was a beautiful scene. Just weeks ago, he'd been living on the east coast with a view of the Atlantic Ocean. Not many would ever experience a coastal life, and he was going to do it on both coasts in a relatively short period.

As he walked, an elderly couple approached him. They held hands and smiled, their eyes drifting to the beach and the setting sun. Both were dressed nicely, perhaps on their way to dinner. The man wore a newsboy cap, and the woman wore a purple bell-shaped hat.

Owen smiled at them. "Evening," he said.

The woman's brow furrowed, and she glanced at her husband. He, in turn, averted his eyes from the big man.

"Say something, Harold."

"Ruffian," the old man muttered.

"Ruffian," she tutted, and they hurried along.

He watched them walk away. That was a reaction he was used to as a Satan's Dawg, but he'd hoped he had moved past it with his new haircut and change in clothing. Although, jeans and a T-shirt probably didn't give him the respectable look he'd previously had while in Maine.

Owen passed several stores that sold clothing and other touristy knickknacks. Most proudly displayed items that read *California* or *Costa Buena* in efforts to separate travelers from their hard-earned dollars.

He passed Seaside Surf Gear, a rental company. A long-haired man quietly waxed the bottom of a surfboard. Owen smiled and nodded. The long-haired man ignored the gesture of kindness and returned his attention to his work.

At Costa Buena Chillers, the bright restaurant was full of screaming children and harried parents. He continued without so much as a second glance.

Several restaurants had open walls so customers could see the view of the ocean as they ate. Even for an autumn day, most were packed with patrons hoping to dine with a view of the beautiful sunset. The fullest establishment was Grill, You Know It's True, a small diner.

Several of the bars along the boardwalk were also starting to fill. The Babble was full of well-dressed patrons.

At Bart's Place, he noticed the hipster who bought The Kinks album sitting alone. Owen paused for a moment to watch a waitress approach the man. The hipster pointed to a table covered with dirty dishes, and she hurried off to begin clearing it.

For a moment, Owen thought about going inside and grabbing a beer. But the allure of drinking himself into a stupor and finding a woman for the night no longer held the same appeal as it once did.

Something had changed for him during his brief stay in Maine.

He met Daphne Winterbourne, a woman unlike any he'd ever met before.

It wasn't that she was attractive, although she certainly was. As Beauregard Smith, he had met many pretty women in his life, but they had never caused him to want to change his life.

And it wasn't that she was smart, which she most definitely was. He'd met a few intelligent women, although admittedly not many. Smart ladies would never give Beau Smith the time of day.

It was that Daphne brought out a goodness in him that he didn't know existed while he lived his life as Beau Smith. It was a goodness Owen wanted to hold on to—that he wanted to share with her.

He'd spent most of his life in, and surrounded by, darkness. It started with his mother, but he embraced it by his actions. When he joined the Satan's Dawgs, and they discovered his talents, the darkness went deeper. So deep, in fact, that he believed there was never a chance for him to get out.

Maybe that's why he agreed to provide information for the FBI.

At first, he convinced himself that he did it to protect his grandmother, the only person he truly loved in his life but becoming a rat allowed him a way out.

He no longer had to be in the dark. Even if he was to spend the rest of his life in prison, he could be free of the things that haunted his thoughts.

His new house was a one-bedroom bungalow at the end of a row of similar structures. They were a half block off the beach and painted in the same bright hues as the boardwalk buildings. In front of the house was a dented Toyota Tercel, courtesy of the U.S. Marshals.

After making a bowl of ramen noodles, Owen sat with a pen and paper to compose a letter.

He'd written letters to his grandmother while he was in prison. This would be the first time he ever wrote to someone other than her.

The pen hovered over the paper. According to the marshals, he wasn't supposed to communicate with anyone from his past. Maybe he could write the letter then throw it away. Perhaps that would make him feel good enough to fill the hole in his heart.

He lowered his head and started to write.

But he stopped after just a few words.

If he was going to do that—throw the letter away—why even write it in the first place? He might as well stuff his feelings back where they belonged.

That's what the old version of himself would do.

And if he did that, he might as well go to the bar, have a beer, and bring home a female companion for the evening.

He didn't want to do that, though. That's not who he wanted to be anymore.

If he wanted to change himself, he needed to take a stand. It didn't have to be a major one, just an act of defiance to the person he used to be. It would show he was a better man than Beauregard Smith, bookkeeper.

It would show the road he was on was worth the pain of loneliness.

His pen touched the paper, and he began the letter.

Chapter 7

"Where were you last night?"

Costa Buena Detective Roy Cochran folded his arms, waiting for Owen's answer.

"At my house."

The detective eyed the uniformed officer standing next to him. His name tag read Santiago. The policeman shrugged under the investigator's gaze.

"Where is your house exactly?" Cochran asked.

"Around the way," Owen said, thumbing in the general direction of where he lived.

"What part of exactly didn't you understand?" the detective asked.

Owen clucked his tongue, then recited his address. He also added, "It's the last bungalow at the end of the block."

The detective unfolded his arms, studied Owen once more, then jotted the address into his notepad.

Roy Cochran wore a tweed sport coat, a white shirt, and blue Dockers. The collar of his shirt remained buttoned, but his tie hung loose and askew. His suede Hush Puppies were scuffed. A husky man, Cochran's face purpled as he wrote. The color faded from his cheeks when he lifted his head to look at Owen again.

"Anybody there to corroborate your story?"

Owen glanced between the detective and the uniformed officer. "You still haven't told me why you're here."

Irritated by Owen's response, Cochran folded his arms again. "You're a shifty type, aren't you?"

"Until I know what's going on, why should I answer your questions?"

The detective sniffed then rubbed a finger under his nose. "Did you have a run-in with Albert Ferguson yesterday?"

Owen's eyes narrowed. "Big Al? You know I did; otherwise, you wouldn't be here. What's he saying I did?"

The detective bent his head to write in his notebook.

"Listen," Owen said, "he hit me. There was a witness to the altercation. Some hipster type. I think he might manage Bart's Place."

"We know."

"You do?"

Officer Santiago nodded in agreement.

"We do," Cochran said when he looked up from his notebook. "We've talked with him."

"What did he say?"

"He said Al hit you."

Owen spread his hands as if vindicated by the truth. "There you go."

"Then you said, and I quote, I owe you one. That true?"

"That's what the guy told us," Santiago offered.

Cochran smirked at the patrolman. "I know that, Chaco. Thank you. I was asking big slim here if it was true."

Santiago glanced away.

"Maybe, I did say that," Owen said, "I don't remember. The guy slugged me, and I wanted to—"

When both the detective and officer leaned in, the hair on the back of Owen's neck stood on end. He immediately stopped talking.

"What did you want to do?" Cochran asked.

He realized then that the cops weren't there because of the fight inside his shop. He was the victim in that situation, and he never retaliated. They were there for something entirely different.

"Nothing."

"You wanted to do nothing?" the detective asked. "That doesn't make any sense."

"He hit me, and I wanted to call the cops, but I figured I'd let it slide."

The detective wiped his finger under his nose a couple of times before saying, "You figured you'd take care of it yourself is more like it."

Something happened to Al Ferguson, Owen thought. *And they suspect me of it.*

Cochran's gaze dropped to Owen's tattoos. His head bent to his notebook, and he made several entries. "Some of those look like prison tats."

They were, but there was no way the detective could know that for sure.

"I paid for these," Owen said.

"With what?" Cochran asked. "Smokes?"

"I'm done talking."

"Owen Hunter," Cochran muttered as he read from his notepad. "Funny as I've never heard of you."

"Why would you?"

"Big guy like you sort of stands out. Especially with prison tats."

"They're not—"

"We should have crossed paths at one time or another. Don't you think? Costa Buena isn't that big of a town."

"I'm new here."

"Figures. When did you arrive?"

He couldn't lie about this as it could be easily disproved. Owen didn't know what they suspected him of, but getting caught in a lie would not be a good way to defend himself. "I got here a couple of days ago. Yesterday was my first in the shop."

"First day in the shop?" Cochran muttered. "And you get yourself into a fight."

Officer Chaco Santiago sneered. "Your first day in town, and we catch a homicide."

"A homicide?" Owen said.

"Think it's a coincidence your competitor was murdered right after you arrive in town?" Cochran leaned in. "Right after you two argue. Right after he assaults you."

"How did he die?"

"You should know," the detective said.

"I didn't kill anyone."

The orange cat ambled out among the three men. It turned a few circles before disappearing back under a rack.

Cochran studied the big man. "The fight was over you improperly changing your business to compete with Big Al—"

"How was it improper? There was never a written agreement."

"Oh, want to talk about written agreements? That's great. Let's talk about how you came into ownership of this here establishment."

"How is that relevant?"

The detective pointed his pen at the big man. "*I'll* decide what's relevant."

"If you've got enough to charge me—" Owen said, but the detective held up his hand, stopping him.

The cat zoomed out from under a rack and sat.

"Save it, tough guy. How'd you get this business so fast?"

"What?"

The detective glanced at the officer, who was now petting the cat. "I stutter, Chaco?"

"No, sir," the officer said. "I heard you perfectly clear."

Cochran turned back to Owen. "The old owner of this business drowned. I know because I was called out on it. A suspicious death and all."

"How is drowning suspicious?" Owen said.

"The man was a known surfer, even at such an advanced age. He'd been doing it for decades. One day he washes up on shore in his wet suit. His surfboard is hooked to his leg. He's got a nasty gash on his head, although it doesn't look like there is any damage to the board. Coroner rules that he drowned. That he had water in his lungs. All evidence points to a freak accident. I got no reason to believe it was anything but bad luck." The detective glanced at the officer then went back to Owen. "Until now, that is."

"What's that mean?"

When the cat bolted back under a rack, Officer Santiago stood.

"Maybe you had something to do with it."

"I didn't even know Costa Buena existed until recently."

"Uh-huh," Cochran said. "I'm gonna do a little more homework on you, maybe pull Prescott Honeywell's file, that's the previous owner of this business—"

"I know who he was."

"—and see if I can make a connection between you two."

"There is a connection. I'm here in the store."

"You know what I mean," Cochran said. He bent his head to jot in his notebook. His face purpled as he did. When he looked up, he said, "Until then, don't go nowhere. Understand?"

"It's a free country."

Cochran eyed Owen's tattoos. "Not for you."

A small ball rolled out from under one of the display racks, followed by the cat. Santiago knelt to look at it.

"You can't stop me from going where I want," Owen said.

The detective smiled. "Wanna try me?"

"Hey, Detective," Santiago said.

"What?"

"Take a look at this."

"What is it?"

"See what the cat is playing with?"

Owen bent over. "That's Elvis's head."

Both men turned and looked at him. Detective Roy Cochran smiled. "Put the cuffs on him, Chaco. We've got our man."

Chapter 8

"Albert Ferguson was killed with an Elvis Presley statue. We recovered the base, but not the head. We searched the premises, but never located it. So imagine our surprise to see this here."

With a gloved hand, Roy Cochran carefully picked up the statue's head and dropped it into a clear plastic bag. Officer Santiago had run out to his car to collect the murder weapon.

"You're going to be disappointed, Detective," Owen said. "Some punk broke that statue in my store."

"Convenient story."

"But it's true."

"That so? Where's the rest of the statue?"

Owen sighed. "It shattered. I threw the rest of it away."

"But you kept the head? Either you take me as a fool, or you've got some small head fetish."

"Neither. I couldn't find that piece after the statue broke. It exploded. There were pieces everywhere. I did my best to pick it up."

The detective smirked. "Humpty Dumpty and all."

"Exactly."

"So, where's the rest of the statue?"

"It might still be in the back. I put it in the trash last night."

Cochran eyed him for a moment. "Stay here."

Owen turned to show his handcuffed hands. "Where am I going?"

The detective walked to the back of the store. When he returned, he smirked. "Trash can's empty. Your convenient story puts you on thinner and thinner ice."

"I promise, Detective. Find the skate punk. Bald guy. Late twenties. All sorts of piercings in his face. Guy tried to extort me, and I told him no. So he broke the statue in retaliation."

"You want me to trust the word of someone you claim committed a felony?"

"If it keeps me out of jail, yes."

The cat sat in the middle of the store, contently watching both men.

Cochran rubbed the side of his face while he thought.

"What do we do now?" Owen asked.

"We wait for Santiago to return with the statue. Then we put the king of rock and roll's head back in place and finger you for the murder."

The big man inhaled deeply. He silently prayed the head from his Elvis statue would not fit neatly together on the one from Al Ferguson's homicide. If so, his days of freedom would quickly end.

"What's the cat's name?" Cochran asked.

Owen didn't feel like making idle chatter with the detective but knew being friends with a police officer was better than being argumentative, especially in moments when you were handcuffed. It was time to make pleasant, he decided. "You get to pick his name."

The detective raised an eyebrow. "How's that?"

He shrugged. "It's sort of a metaphysical thing. You see, cats are a reflection of the person they're with at any time. Therefore, a person should be able to name the cat."

Cochran pursed his lips then said. "Interesting."

"But there are a couple of rules to the naming."

"Such as?"

"He has to be named after a musician."

"Doable."

"And no cute names."

"No cute names. And it has to be named after a musician."

"That's it?" Cochran said. "I can name him whatever I want?"

"Whatever you want. He'll be a reflection of you."

"In that case, I'm gonna call him Possum."

"Possum? What the heck is that?"

"That was George Jones's nickname."

"George Jones?"

"The country singer."

"I meant rock musician."

"You didn't say that."

"Do I look like a guy who wants my cat named after a country musician?"

"But I followed your rules," Cochran said. "Exactly as described."

He stared at the detective. What was it with these people from California? Couldn't they understand a simple naming rule? Why'd they have to go and make it so hard?

Officer Santiago came back into the store with a brown paper bag. He had a light sheen of sweat on his forehead.

"Here you go, Detective."

"Now," Cochran said, "let's see you wriggle your way out of this."

The detective stuck his hand into the small sack and pulled out a headless statue of Elvis. He set it on the counter and stepped back.

The statue's body wore a white jumpsuit and had a guitar strapped over its swollen belly. He kneeled with both arms spread wide. Only the head was missing.

"Now, for the proof," the detective said, pulling the clear plastic bag from his pocket.

With his hands handcuffed behind his back, Owen interlocked his fingers as if praying.

The three men—Cochran, Santiago, and Owen—leaned in toward the counter as the detective gently placed Elvis's head onto the top of his body.

For a moment, it stayed in place, then it teetered over and clattered to the glass top counter.

Cochran grunted, picked it up, and tried again. He wiggled it slowly left and right, but the head never fit correctly into the statue's base.

"Hmm," the detective said as he fiddled further with the head.

Owen's heart raced with every passing second.

Eventually, Cochran placed a fingertip on top of Elvis's head to hold it in place. He leaned back to get a better angle of view. Santiago and Owen joined him.

The head was too small for the statue, and it appeared too thin for the body below.

Owen straightened and smiled.

"It's not the right Elvis head," Cochran muttered. "This one goes to a different statue."

"Two Elvis heads?" Santiago asked.

He turned and presented his hands to the officer. "You owe me an apology."

When the handcuffs slipped off, Santiago slipped them back into the case on his belt.

"Just because the head didn't fit, doesn't mean you're not a suspect," Cochran said.

"How about if the head doesn't fit, you must acquit?" Owen smiled.

The detective smirked. "Different Cochran. And you could have broken off the head of your statue to throw us off guard."

"Uh-huh. That sounds reasonable," Owen said. "You really think I did that?"

Cochran squinted as he thought. When he finally made up his mind, he said, "Maybe not, but right now, you're still my best suspect. You had the most to gain by getting Big Al Ferguson out of the way. I'm keeping my eye on you, Mr. Hunter."

The detective put the headless Elvis statue back into the brown paper bag. Then he took a final look at the small head of the king of rock and roll that lay on the glass counter.

"We almost got ahead in this case," he muttered.

"Really?" Owen said.

Officer Santiago smirked. "Might have worked if we hadn't lost our heads."

"All right," Owen said, lifting his hands. "That's enough. Can I get back to work, please?"

Chapter 9

"Ace Adventures, where your journey begins. How may I help you?"

Owen held the phone tightly to his ear as an older woman entered Rockafellers. She wore a purple fedora. Its floppy brim bounced as she moved through the store.

"This is Owen Hunter," he said to the woman on the other end of the line. "I'm already a customer."

The woman briefly eyed Owen as she headed toward a display table labeled *Jazz*.

Over the phone, he could hear the clicking of a keyboard. "Oh, yes, Mr. Hunter. I see it right here. How is California this time of year, sir?"

He knew the operator would have traced the call to his exact location and would be reviewing his case file right now. The Ace Adventures cover was how the U.S. Marshals created a way for him to contact them in the event there was ever a problem.

"It's cool."

"That's great. I've never been to—"

"As in, not warm."

"Oh," the operator said. "I would have expected—"

"Is Mr. Onderdonk available? I want to speak about my vacation plans."

The keyboard clicking returned. "He's currently with another customer. I can have him call you back later."

"Please do so."

"May I tell him what this is in regard to?"

Owen watched the woman pet the cat. As she did, her eyes flicked to him.

"I need to cancel my reservation."

"Any specific reason?"

The woman stood and stretched her back, rolling her head toward Owen. Her eyes were intense with interest.

"I'll explain when he calls."

After Owen hung up the phone, the woman moved toward the counter.

"Mr. Hunter, I presume?"

The cat rubbed against her leg.

"Yes."

She held out a slender, almost delicate hand. "Marlene Babb."

Owen's hand carefully enveloped hers. "What can I do for you?"

"On the contrary, it's what I can do for you." The way she said it sounded like Sam the Scavenger.

When the big man released her hand, she held onto to him for a moment longer, her grip belying his earlier belief of frailty.

"Which is what, exactly?"

She waved a hand around his store. "I'd like to buy your building *and* your business. I'll pay top dollar. More than anyone else, I can assure you."

"They're not for sale."

"Honey, haven't you heard? Everything is for sale. You only have to find the right price."

"Not this."

A seriousness descended on the woman's face. "Said the man without a customer in his store."

"You're here."

"To buy your building."

"I'm changing the format of the business. That'll bring in new customers."

"I heard. You're planning to compete with Headbangers."

How did she hear that news? Owen wondered.

At first, only Sam knew his plans. But a couple of others had learned of them since then. Big Al, but he was dead. And the hipster knew. Regardless of who told Marlene, word traveled fast in Costa Buena.

"Lucky for you that your competitor should end up dead one day after deciding to change your store's format."

"I had nothing to do with that."

Marlene nodded. "I didn't say you did, dear. Although, weren't the police talking with you earlier?"

"You sure know a lot about what's going around here."

"I should. I own most of it."

"Most of what?"

"The boardwalk. My husband, bless his heart, and God rest his soul, worked hard to acquire every parcel. For the better part of fifty years, he did. And he almost reached that goal, except one."

"This one?"

"That's right. So how much do you want for it?"

"As I said, it's not for sale."

Marlene's eyes narrowed. "But we—I want it."

"We?"

"Bad habit," Marlene said. "I miss my husband."

"I'm sorry for your loss, and it's not for sale."

The woman put a hand on the counter and leaned in. She pushed her purple hat up slightly so she could study his eyes. Then her attention dropped to his hands. "Why are you selling this moldy old stuff? Your hands are too rough for this type of work. You seem better suited to mechanic's work. Or maybe a fighter of some sort. Selling Rat Pack records doesn't suit you. Even if you change the decade, peddling albums won't make you wealthy."

"Money isn't all it's cracked up to be." Even to him, the words rang hollow.

Marlene laughed. "Oh dear, if money isn't what it's cracked up to be, then why do any of this?"

She turned to leave the store but stopped and turned back to him. "You seem to be the type who puts all his eggs in one basket."

"What's that mean?"

"Be careful someone doesn't take your basket, or you'll be left without any eggs."

She chuckled as she walked out of the store.

Chapter 10

The door swung slightly open, and Samuel Peyton leaned his shoulder into it to push it wider. In his hands, he held a plastic milk crate filled with albums. Even though it was chilly outside, he still wore no shirt. The only difference from his first visit was he had exchanged his flip-flops for a ratty pair of tennis shoes.

Owen walked over to the counter to meet him.

"Got you some records, Hunter," Sam said. His words strained from the weight in his hands. After he lifted the crate onto the counter, he continued. "Got a bit of everything. There's some more out in my van."

The big man flipped through the albums. There were names of classic bands he knew— AC/DC, Aerosmith, Alice Cooper, The Animals, Black Sabbath, Blondie, David Bowie, James Brown.

The orange tom ambled out from under a display rack and approached the visitor. Sam bent over and scratched behind his ear. "Yerchoise, how ya doin', buddy?"

"These are pretty good," the big man said.

When Sam straightened, the cat wandered off. He smiled. "I told you I could get the good stuff."

On the corner of several albums were lime green price tags.

"Where'd you get these?" Owen asked as his thumb rubbed one of the tags.

"There's a thrift store in Rancho Chimera that got a big order in. I've got a connection who sells to me before they ever hit the floor. Pennies on the dollar."

Owen considered what he said. He wasn't sure where Rancho Chimera was, but most California cities sounded the same.

"He lets me pick what I want," Sam continued. "Those I pass over get put out for the diggers and the online sellers to scrounge through."

"All right," the big man said. "How much?"

"Fifty cents apiece?"

When Owen nodded, Sam rubbed his hands together. "Papa's gonna eat good tonight."

"But before you get the rest..."

"Yeah?" the half-naked man asked expectantly.

"You told Al about me changing my format."

Sam's smile vanished, and he swallowed hard.

"Why'd you do that?"

The visitor grabbed his long braid and tugged on it, turning his head while he spoke. "Al was good people. I thought he should know he was gonna have competition in town."

"Good people? He came in here and punched me."

"He punched you?"

"Right here." Owen tapped Sam twice on the side of the chin. "I figure you owe me for that."

The rotund man blanched. "Sure. I can see how you could figure that. A pain and suffering sort of thing."

"You're smarter than you look."

"People have been saying that for years. So, how can I make this right?"

"For starters, you can give me a fifty percent discount on our agreed-upon price."

The U.S. Marshals would ensure Rockafellers remained successful, so it didn't matter if he made a profit, but Owen wanted to show he could operate a legitimate business. The Satan's Dawgs had run a series of scams, some successful, some not. He'd learned a few business practices from being around them. As the club's bookkeeper, though, he didn't participate in those activities. His specialty was the removal of club problems.

But now he was looking for a new challenge. Turning a profit with a vintage record store seemed a fine way to entertain himself.

"Fifty percent?" Sam whined. "Ten."

"Ten and I get to punch you," Owen said. "In the same spot Big Al hit me." He tapped Sam on the chin again.

The rotund man whitened further. "Fifty percent, but just this time."

He pretended to think about it, but he would have taken any deal. He only wanted to get a discount out of the man to see if he could do it. "Fine," Owen said.

Sam exhaled, and his shoulders slumped. "I'll get the other crates."

"Hold up."

The scavenger's eyes widened. "What *now?*"

"Marlene Babb. What do you know about her?"

Sam glanced at the box of albums. "I'll tell you what. You can have those. Let's call it good."

Owen grabbed Sam's sweaty arm. "Where are you going? We're still talking."

The smaller man stared at the ceiling. "I don't want no part of whatever you got going with her."

"Why not? What's so special about Marlene Babb?"

"She's bad news is what she is."

"How do you know?"

"Me and her, we had some history before she hooked up with Bartholomew Babb."

"Who's he?"

"He used to be my friend before she got her claws into him. He owned a couple of bars and buildings on the boardwalk. She saw an opportunity to trade up, and she took it."

"You mean Bart's Place?" Owen asked, thinking about the bar he had stopped in front of on his way home the previous evening.

Sam nodded. "And The Babble, too. He started Bart's Place back in the early sixties, I believe. He opened Babble not too long after. Bought both buildings for close to a song. Costa Buena wasn't a tourist destination back then. Heck, I don't think California was that big of a deal then, either."

"Marlene said Bart bought up everything along the boardwalk."

Sam slowly nodded his head. "He did it 'cause of her. She was twenty years younger than the man, but she rode him like a rented mule. Bart never knew what hit him. After he said, 'I do,' the poor guy never got another day off in his life."

"You knew him pretty well?"

"As good as a man could, I guess. He used to tend bar at Bart's. That was my joint after I'd get off work back when I was a wage slave, not the free man you see before you now." He rubbed his stomach. "Anyway, ol' Bart would tell me how Marlene kept his nose to the grindstone, forcing him to make more and more money to buy up more and more properties."

"You said you were friends."

"At first, we were friends because we had something in common—he poured my drinks, and I drank them. After Marlene latched onto him, we stayed friends because we shared a common misery."

"She wants to buy my building."

Sam sheepishly looked away.

"What?"

"Sell it to her. Take your money and run. Talk around the boardwalk is she ain't none too happy you bought this out from under her."

"How do you know that?"

"I hear things."

"Who did you hear it from?"

"Everybody. Everybody's talking about it. Ol' Prescott, the guy who owned the business before you, agreed to sell it to her. Guess it was a handshake deal for whenever he decided to call it a day. I asked Prescott about it once, and he said he agreed to sell it just to get her to leave him alone. He said, 'What do I care? I'll be dead.'"

Sam continued. "I guess they never got anything officially put in writing. I think Marlene was trying to get something signed and then Prescott up and drowned. Threw her whole plan off. To make matters worse, you showed up. She's spittin' nails about it."

Owen rubbed his chin as he thought. "She didn't seem mad about it."

"The lady hides her emotions well. Believe me."

"Sounds like you know her pretty well."

"As I said, we go back. Let's leave it at that."

"How did she know I was changing my concept to compete with Headbangers?"

"I didn't tell her." Sam raised his right hand. "I'd never tell that woman anything. I'd swear to that on a stack of Beatles albums. You can take that to the bank, Hunter."

The big man scratched his face. "You mentioned Prescott's drowning. What do you know about it?"

Sam dropped his hand and shook his head. "Surprised us all. The guy was a decent shredder, you know?"

"Shredder?"

"Of the waves."

"He really surfed? At his age?"

"Age is only a number, man. Believe me. You'll change your attitude once you get some gray on the peak. Anyway, it was one of those freak accidents that happen sometimes. Guess it was the universe's way of saying it was his time to return to the origins of space and time."

"Was it like him to surf alone?"

"Totally. The guy was a bit of a loner. Nice enough, but never really needed anyone. Not sure how he could do it, actually."

"What? Surf?"

"And swim out there in the ocean. I'm more of a sand and sun guy myself. Afraid of the sharks and other things lurking below the surface."

Owen's brow furrowed as he considered the man's words. Finally, he said, "All right, Sam. Let's keep any business just between us from now on?"

"Yeah, for sure. Can I go get the other boxes?"

The big man nodded absently as his thoughts had returned to Marlene Babb and how she knew so much about his business.

Chapter 11

Three of them angrily filed into the store, led by a skate punk wearing the sleeveless army jacket. It was the same punk from the other day.

"That's him," he said, pointing to Owen as he knelt over a box.

He'd been flipping through the albums he'd just purchased from Sam the Scavenger. In his hand was an album he couldn't believe Sam the Scavenger had tried to slip by him. He would have never allowed it in his store.

Two punks flanked their leader, set their feet, and clenched their fists. They scowled menacingly at Owen.

To the left was a rail of a man with a high, green mohawk. He wore a leather vest over a black T-shirt with a large red A covered with a circle—the symbol for anarchy. His torn and tattered jeans were tucked inside untied combat boots.

To the leader's right was a short, pale man with a limp afro covered by the hoodie of an unzipped sweatshirt. The garment dangled precariously from his shoulders, exposing his T-shirt, which read *The Future is Dead*.

Still holding the record in his hand, Owen straightened and moved toward the three men.

"Where's my board?" the apparent leader of the group demanded.

"Yeah, where's his board?" the rail-thin guy echoed.

Eying his compatriots, the one in the hoodie remained silent.

Owen pointed to the wall behind the counter.

Above the Mötley Crüe poster hung the skateboard. This morning, after mailing the letter he wrote to Daphne Winterbourne, Owen placed it there right before the police arrived to accuse him of murdering Big Al Ferguson.

"What's it doing up there?" the bald punk whined.

"Yeah, what's it—"

Leader jerked his head, and Rail stopped speaking. Hoodie rolled his eyes.

"It's a trophy," the big man said.

"A trophy?" Leader moaned. "Get it down."

Owen's eyes dropped to the album in his hands. If he didn't retrieve the skateboard, he knew what would happen now—there would be a fight. However, if he relented and got the skateboard, then he showed he could be intimidated. They would again demand their protection money—money he already refused to pay.

He saw only one option, but it violated a rule set by Marshal Onderdonk.

Do not develop habits from your old life.

"You deaf?" Leader sneered. "I said, get it down."

"Yeah," Rail joined in, "you deaf?"

Without further hesitation, Owen ferociously slapped Leader with the album, breaking the record inside, and folding the cardboard cover in two.

With his left hand, the big man punched Rail in the nose. The tall man squeaked and brought his hands up to his face as blood spurted onto his lips. He stumbled backward until he tripped over his own feet and crumbled to the floor.

Leader, recovering from the initial surprise of the record slap, stepped forward and drew his fist back. Owen kicked him in the shin, causing the man to look down. The big man threw a right hook to the punk's chin, which corkscrewed him into the ground.

Frozen during the melee was Hoodie, his eyes glued to his fallen leader. When Owen now moved toward him, his hands shot up in the air. He blurted, "I give."

Owen's face warmed as he considered striking the smaller man. "Still demanding protection money?"

"Not me," Hoodie said, shaking his head. The front part of his blond afro bounced wildly.

"Others on the boardwalk actually pay what you demand?"

He shrugged. "Some do."

The bigger man pointed to Leader. "When he wakes up, tell him I'll never pay. Got it?"

Hoodie lowered his hands. "Yeah, yeah, man, I got it."

"Get them out of my store before I call the cops."

Before I call the cops, Owen thought ruefully. He would never call the police.

As the bookkeeper for the Satan's Dawgs, he would have made these punks regret crossing him. At a minimum, they would have required extended stays in a local hospital. The leader, having not learned from his first transgression, might have been dealt with permanently. But Owen was trying to change and be a better man.

Daphne quickly passed through his mind. When she learned of his background, it confused her, as it conflicted with the image he projected. He wanted—no, he needed—for her to know he was no longer a Dawg. Or at least, he was trying not to be.

After Hoodie assisted Rail to the front of the store, he returned for Leader. He struggled to drag the fallen man out of the store.

Owen picked up the broken album, Captain and Tennille's *Greatest Hits*. He frowned when he saw the song "Muskrat Love" listed on the back of the album. He considered demanding a refund from Sam for sneaking that record *into* his store but smacking the punk with it had been an enjoyable way to use the record. The big man threw the album in the waste bin.

Through the window, Owen watched the three punks huddling on the boardwalk. Leader swayed badly and placed his arm around Hoodie's shoulders. Rail leaned his head back to stop the blood flowing from his nose.

Chapter 12

The door burst open, and Anita Moffett stalked in, her face pinched. She wore a dark green pantsuit. A clip pulled her hair back from her face.

"What is that?" she demanded.

"What?" Owen asked.

"That," she pointed out the window to the three punks. They stood in the middle of the boardwalk, holding onto each other, commiserating about the fight they'd just been in.

A group of onlookers stood around the three men. Several took photos with their cell phones.

"We had a disagreement. I have a right to refuse service to anyone."

"No, you do not," Anita said. "You most certainly do not. That was in the brochure. Did you not read it?"

"I read it." In fact, he hadn't read it. After barely skimming the brochure, he threw it in the trash.

"Then you know you're supposed to serve everyone," Anita said. Her tone took on that of a scolding mother. "That's a duty and responsibility of every business in Costa Buena."

"I don't agree."

"You don't agree?" She stared at him, aghast. Then she shook her head firmly. "You don't get to make that choice."

"I don't?"

"No, Mr. Owen, you most certainly do not. As a business owner in Costa Buena, you are supposed to welcome all people, whether they be residents or visitors to our community. It's your duty, your responsibility, to accommodate everyone who walks through your door."

"But—"

She held up a hand to interrupt him. "Costa Buena is striving to be a guiding light, not only for California but for the nation and the world. If you want to do business here, then you must pick up that mantle and join us in leading the way. You need to be a beacon of hope."

"I run a used record store. I don't want to be a beacon of any sort."

Her lip curled. "That's what Albert Ferguson would say. Don't be like him."

"Al didn't like your community activism?"

"It's not activism, Mr. Owen. It's community caring. Some of us care for the community. Those who don't are welcome to leave."

"Like Al and me."

"We'd prefer it if you worked to get along with the community."

"I'm not trying to cause problems; I just want to sell some records."

"That's fine, but in Costa Buena, we expect you to do it a certain way. We granted you a business license and, unless you act accordingly, we can take it away."

"Are you with the government?"

"I'm with the people," Anita said. "What's so hard to understand? Start acting like you want to be one of us."

Owen pointed out the window. "Those pillars of the community that you want me to serve were shaking me down."

"Shaking you down? Those boys? I doubt it."

"They demanded I pay them protection money like they were some boardwalk mobsters. Believe it."

She smirked. "Protection from who? From what?"

"From them."

Anita looked at the three men outside the window. Leader and Rail were now angrily pointing at Hoodie. It appeared they were upset he hadn't been assaulted the same way that they had.

"They wouldn't hurt you," Anita said. "Two of those boys are locals. Been here since they were kids. The third one, I don't know, but I'm sure if you took the time to get to know them—"

"Get to know them? I do know them. When I was a kid, I used to be them."

"Then you shouldn't have refused them service. You should have reached out to them—"

"Listen, lady, they—"

"*Anita.* My name is Anita. You need to respect all visitors to your store, or I will revoke your business license."

Owen held his hands in mock surrender. "*Anita*, I apologize. I'm telling you, those three are bad news."

"And I'm telling you that they're just misunder—"

She turned to face the window as Leader and Rail both struck Hoodie. The smaller man tumbled to the ground while the other two kicked at him.

The group of onlookers stayed where they were. Many photographed the melee.

"Oh!" Anita exclaimed. "You have to do something."

Owen chuckled. "I already did. I kicked them out of my store. They're no longer my problem."

Anita faced him with a look of exasperation. She lifted her hands in resignation, then ran outside. The woman waved her arms and yelled at the two men assaulting Hoodie.

She then pleaded with the crowd to help her stop the fight, but none moved to assist her. Instead, many in the crowd took her picture.

Finally, Leader and Rail stopped kicking Hoodie and glowered at her. She took several steps back. When the two men stepped toward her, she pointed at Rockafellers.

Both men stopped, looked around her, and into the window. Owen waved at them.

Leader and Rail sneered at Anita before lifting Hoodie to his feet. As the three of them ambled down the boardwalk, several in the crowd continued to photograph the punks.

Anita shook her head as she stomped back toward the shop.

When she stepped inside, Owen said brightly, "Welcome to Rockafellers, where the music never dies."

She stopped and furrowed her brow. "I was just in here."

The big man forced a wide smile. "I know, but I wanted to make you feel welcomed back. You said I needed to be more accommodating."

Her face reddened. "*You.*"

The cat strolled out to see who was in the store. He wandered over to the woman and rubbed against her leg. She bent to pet the cat.

"Nikki likes you."

"Nikki?"

He thumbed toward the Mötley Crüe poster hanging behind the counter. "He's the grumpy one."

Anita eyed the poster of the four angry men with clenched fists. She turned back to Owen, slightly shaking her head. "He's Cat Stevens. You said."

"You have to pick a new name every time you come in," Owen said.

Her eyes widened. "Since when?"

"It's a new rule," Owen said. "I figured it would be more fun."

"Not for the cat."

"It's just a cat," Owen said. "How would it even know?"

"It?" Anita's ears reddened now. "You—" she stammered, "you are a vile person, treating a cat that way. You obviously do not want to fit into this community."

"Wait. Aren't you supposed to be welcoming, too?"

She pointed at Owen. "You are! You're the business." She tapped her chest. "I'm the *people*."

With that, she yanked the door open and hurried down the boardwalk.

The big man smiled at the cat. "It's okay, Travis. I'm not changing your name." He had named the tom while in Pleasant Valley and had no intention of renaming him now.

Travis rubbed against the big man's leg.

"But that doesn't mean I like you," Owen said.

The cat stopped and eyed him.

Chapter 13

"You're certainly developing a reputation, and it's only your second day."

"Wasn't my intention," Owen said.

The hipster had returned and now stood in front of the *R* section, flipping lazily through the albums. He wore the same outfit as before—a short-sleeved white shirt, tight black jeans, and black loafers.

"Didn't help that you told the cops about my run-in with Al Ferguson."

The hipster glanced back at him. "Are you upset by that?"

"How'd they find you so quickly? How would they know we even talked?"

"I went to them when I saw a commotion at Headbangers."

"You went to them?" Owen asked.

"Sure," he said as he continued to flip through the records. "I figured something bad had happened, and I wanted to know what."

"And you offered up our conversation? The fact Al and I had an altercation."

The hipster shrugged. "I only told them the truth. Besides, I didn't figure you to be the one that did him any harm."

"How would you figure that after only meeting me once?"

"You seem smart enough not to threaten a man in front of a stranger, only to go and kill him later." He studied something on an album cover. "I even told the cops that, too."

"You did, huh?"

"I did."

"They don't seem to share your same assessment of my mental faculties."

"They're cops," he said, flipping through a new row of albums. "If they could do anything else, don't you think they'd be doing it?"

That wasn't a comment Owen would have expected from the clean-cut hipster. He watched the younger man for a moment further before turning his attention back to the crates of albums Sam the Scavenger brought him.

Before the visitor arrived, Owen was inventorying the new works. As he listed the titles, he looked up a recommended price online.

Without fail, the green tags stuck to the corner of the albums were within pennies to the recommended sales price. Someone at the thrift store had already done the homework concerning this. He figured a thrift store would have been a little more slapdash to get the product in and out the door. Whoever Sam's friend was had more on the ball than Owen gave them credit for.

"It seems the Welcoming and Standards Committee has taken a special interest in you."

Owen looked up. "You mean Anita?"

The hipster stepped to the records beginning with *S* and continued his search. "Be careful with that one."

"Or she'll bring the weight of the Costa Buena government down on me?"

The younger man met his gaze. "The committee is not the government."

Owen spread his hands. "Thank you. That's what I've been trying to understand."

"They're far more powerful than our local government."

"They?"

"Oh, the Welcoming and Standards Committee is an umbrella organization. It has dozens of members that make up dozens of subcommittees. You have to go along with them if you want to get along in Costa Buena. Understand?"

"Sounds like they're the mob."

"Worse. They're true believers."

"Of what? Government overreach?"

The hipster stopped his search but kept his hand in between a couple of albums. "They believe in the purity of Costa Buena."

"Purity?"

"Sure."

"What's so pure about this place?"

"What's not?" The hipster lifted his chin toward the window. "How about that sunset?"

Across the boardwalk and past the sand, the edge of the horizon was hued with oranges and purples.

Owen shook his head, unimpressed. He turned back to the visitor. "Since the moment I arrived, I've been bullied by the locals, harassed by other businesses, and intimidated by a woman claiming to be with the local government.”

“Anita claimed she was with the government?”

The big man held the hipster’s gaze. The younger man never looked away from the challenge.

“She might give an impression that she’s with the government,” the hipster allowed, “but she never claims such a thing. Am I right?”

Owen didn’t answer but broke their gaze to look at the ceiling.

“And what business harassed you?”

“Headbangers.”

“Did Al harass you for no reason, or did he challenge you because you were selling a product that he believed he had an exclusive agreement to sell? Remember, I was here for that argument.”

The big man’s eyes narrowed. “What did you say you do?”

“Manage people and situations. And who bullied you?”

“Some skate punks,” Owen muttered.

The hipster’s eyes flicked to the skateboard hanging behind the counter. “The three punks who were beat up today? Whose pictures are posted all over local social media accounts? They don’t look like they could bully anyone.”

“They tried.”

The hipster removed his hand from the display box, letting the albums fall back into place. He picked up an album he previously selected and moved toward the counter.

When Owen stood and stretched, the cat appeared from under a display table. It sat in the middle of the store and stared at the big man.

"Didn't take you for a cat person," the hipster said.

"I'm not."

The hipster frowned. "What's its name?"

"You pick."

"You haven't named it yet?"

"A cat is a reflection of the person they're with at that precise moment. Therefore, that person should be able to name the cat."

"Interesting."

"There's only one catch to that rule. It must be named after a musician."

The hipster studied the tom.

"What'd you name the cat?"

"Travis."

The visitor eyed him. "Like Travis Barker from Blink-182?"

With a shrug, Owen said, "That'll work."

The young man squatted to pet the cat. "How are you this evening, Travis?"

"That's my name for the cat. You should select your own."

As soon as the words tumbled from his mouth, he realized how ridiculous it sounded. He didn't even like the cat, and now he was defending the name he selected as something solely his.

Stupid, Owen thought.

"Travis is a perfectly fine name. I'll use it, too. Besides, it's a cat, right?"

Owen's face warmed as the hipster handed him the album, and a couple of bills to cover the cost. Travis was *his* name for the cat. He didn't want this stranger to use it.

The big man worked the register as the visitor turned to the cat once more. "Keep the change," he said and straightened. "Travis. He looks like a Travis, doesn't he? Sort of goofy and big-headed."

The visitor headed toward the front.

Owen said, "Forget something?" He held up The Animals' self-titled album.

The hipster playfully tapped himself on the side of the head. He returned to the counter, grabbed the album, and headed toward the door. With his hand on the doorknob, he turned back toward the big man.

"It was nice talking with you, Owen."

As the door closed, the big man tried to recall when he gave the hipster his name.

Chapter 14

Grill, You Know It's True was so full of customers he was forced to sit at the counter.

A quick survey of the establishment showed only two employees—a short-order cook and a server.

From behind the grill, a small hunched-over man in his early seventies watched him with tired eyes.

The server, a similarly hunched-over man with suspicious eyes, stood in front of him. "What do you want?" he asked.

"Got a menu?" Owen asked.

The server smirked. "One of those types, huh?"

He reached under the counter, pulled out a paper menu, and slid it in front of Owen. He didn't leave then. Instead, he crossed his arms and continued to observe Owen intently.

He slowly opened the crinkled menu, then perused the choices. There weren't a lot of options.

"Can I get a glass of water?" Owen asked.

"When you order, I'll bring you something to drink. What do you want?"

"I haven't made up my mind."

The server uncrossed his arms, put his hands on the edge of the counter, and leaned slightly forward.

Owen thought about leaving, but he glanced around the restaurant. Everyone hungrily ate their dinners. Hardly anyone talked, as they were too busy eating.

"Read the menu," the old man said. "Don't look around."

"What?"

The server thumbed between himself and the short-order cook. "Does it look like me and him have time to waste? Get to orderin'."

Owen consulted the menu once more. "How about a burger and fries?"

"How about?" the server asked. "Is that what you want, or is it not? We ain't takin' it back."

"A burger and fries. I'd like it with—"

The older man snatched the menu from his hands. "He'll make it the way he makes it." He turned and said, "Did you hear—"

"I heard!" the cook yelled and slapped a ball of hamburger on the grill.

The server shook his head and wandered to the end of the counter. He grabbed a glass, filled it with tap water, and returned to Owen. He clunked the glass down in front of the big man.

"Can I get some ice?"

"No ice."

The big man slid the glass to himself. "Your customer service is rough around the edges."

"Need me to hold you?" the old man asked. "Burp you when you're done?"

"What?" Owen said, pulling back. "No."

"Good, because you are here to eat, not be a baby."

The older man folded his arms and studied the customers who ate with their heads down.

None looked his way, and no one seemed to mind his gruff demeanor either.

"Been here a long time?" Owen asked.

"Long enough," the old man mumbled.

"How long?"

The older man scowled at Owen. "Why are you so nosy?"

"I'm new here."

"New, where?"

"Costa Buena. The boardwalk."

The older man's eyes narrowed. "What business do you own?"

"Rockafellers."

"From Prescott, huh?"

"His estate, yeah."

The older man rubbed his chin. "I don't know."

"What don't you know?"

"Prescott. He was different. Something I couldn't put my finger on."

Owen shrugged. "I wouldn't know. I never met the man."

"He was here a lot of years but never had no visitors. No family. Never had himself a woman. Even we," he thumbed toward the short-order cook, "have women. I guess he could've had himself a man, I suppose, but he didn't have one of them either. He was always alone. Secretive."

"Not sure," Owen said. "As I said, I never met the man."

"What about you? You have a woman?"

"Why are you so nosy?" Owen asked.

A smile hinted at the corners of the older man's mouth. He immediately pushed it away and walked off to wipe down a table. A man and a woman entered the restaurant, took the table, and ordered without the help of a menu. When the server returned, he reported the couple's order to the cook.

When the old man stood behind the counter, he asked, "What's your name?"

"Owen."

"Horace," he said. He jerked his head to the cook. "Gerald, my brother."

The older man's eyes swept over the other customers. Satisfied with what he saw, his attention returned to Owen.

"Where'd you come up with the name for the business, Horace?"

"Something wrong with it?"

"Making conversation."

Horace remained silent for several moments before saying. "Our niece. She named it when we opened. Thirty years ago." Horace surveyed the customers before continuing. "Grill is our last name, so it was clever what she did. You like it?"

"Yeah."

"You don't sound so sure," Horace said. Disbelief registered in his eyes.

"Thirty years," Owen said, ignoring the old man's question. "You must have seen some changes on the boardwalk."

"The boardwalk doesn't change. Only the people."

"What about Bartholomew Babb?"

"Ol' Bart." Horace's eyes softened. "Nice man. A saint." Horace made the sign of the cross, kissed his thumb, then lifted it to the sky.

"He owned this building, right?"

"He bought it from our first landlord, but Bart was decent. Always treated us fair. If something broke, he fixed it. Never a cross word the whole time we knew each other."

"What about his wife?"

The older man's face flattened, and he pretended to spit on the floor. "She is... that woman..." He shook his head. "I have nothing nice to say."

"What has she done?"

"What hasn't she done? She won't fix anything when it breaks. She makes us do it. She raises our rent. If we refuse to pay, she says get out, that she'll get a new renter. She's horrible."

"Why not move?"

Horace stared at him. "This is the boardwalk. Where else would we go? Look around. People come here because this is where we are, where we've been. We're too old to start over."

"You're never too old."

"Said the foolish young man with plenty of time ahead."

"What about the community organizers? They seem to want to keep the community a certain way."

"The do-gooders?" Horace laughed loudly.

Several restaurant patrons paused their eating to look his way.

"What's so funny?" Gerald hollered from behind the grill.

"This one," Horace said, jerking his head toward Owen. "He says the do-gooders will help us with Marlene."

Gerald's shoulders bobbed up and down as he chuckled.

Horace turned back to Owen. "Marlene is one of them. She's their sponsor."

"Sponsor?"

The older man looked up as he thought. "Benefactor," he said.

"She's part of their committee?" Owen asked.

"Why do you think they're so focused on keeping us in line? Because Marlene makes them dance like puppets." He mimed moving marionettes with strings. "Going to the do-gooders won't help. We pay what we hafta so we can keep our doors open."

"What about fighting back?"

Horace's eyes slanted. "Fight back?"

"She owns everything on the boardwalk, right?"

"Except for your building. Convenient for this conversation."

"What I'm saying is that if you can get everyone to band together and refuse to pay rent, refuse to deal with her, then you'd have real power."

Horace's face turned white.

"It would be like forming a union with the tenants."

Gerald walked from behind the grill and slid a plate in front of Owen. On it was a beautiful hamburger and a pile of golden-brown French fries. Next to the burger, various sliced vegetables were laid out.

"Thank you," Owen said, taking in the presentation on his plate.

"Go to the do-gooders," the short-order cook muttered as he returned to the kitchen.

Horace leaned in and lowered his voice. "What you're suggesting, it's already been discussed."

"By who?"

"Big Al."

"Al Ferguson? When did he discuss this?"

Horace glanced around before speaking. "For the last couple of weeks, and now he's dead."

"How many people did he tell?"

Horace shrugged. "I don't know. He was only starting to get support among some of the businesses." He looked up and glanced around again. "If I were you, I'd keep that idea to yourself. To be on the safe side."

Chapter 15

Owen lay in bed, his mind whirring with thoughts. He'd only been in Costa Buena for two full days, and he was already a suspect in the murder of his competitor. He thought he cleared himself when young Elvis's head hadn't matched the fat Elvis statue, but Detective Roy Cochran made his position clear—he was going to keep an eye on Owen.

That was not good for him.

Had he not wanted to change the Rockafellers concept, had he left it alone with the dull fifties and sixties music, nothing would ever have happened. He wouldn't have fought with Big Al Ferguson, and Detective Cochran wouldn't be poking around in his life.

Instead, Owen wanted to pursue his dreams.

He wanted to make a change so he could be happy.

What does happiness have to do with anything?

His childhood wasn't happy, not while he lived with Paula, his mother. No, that was an endless series of disappointments. There were flashes of happiness when he visited his grandmother, but they were always bookended by the reality that he would return to his mom.

His teen years weren't any better when his mother and he acted like roommates. They co-existed then, barely talking to each other, only communicating when absolutely necessary. He grew his hair long, got into heavy metal, and discovered that being feared by people was better than being looked down upon. None of that brought him joy, though.

Even when he joined the Satan's Dawgs, the group that became his surrogate family, happiness never entered the equation. He felt safe there, became part of something larger than himself, but a sense of true contentment remained elusive.

Life for him was full of all sorts of emotions—disappointment, regret, sadness, anger, hatred—but happiness never made any lasting stay.

Until he landed in Pleasant Valley.

That's when he learned people could like him for who he was—well, for the person they thought he was. Still, he learned it was better to be liked than feared. Instead of scowls or averted glances, people smiled at him. Rather than diverting their paths, folks wanted to be around him.

And then he met Daphne Winterbourne.

Unfortunately, she knew him as Brody Steele and believed him to be the new owner of a mystery bookstore. She even developed feelings for that person.

Then it all fell apart, and he had to leave.

Owen rubbed his face before clicking on the lamp next to his bed. He stared at the ceiling. Sleep was eluding him tonight with all these thoughts, especially the ones of his recent past. He had to stop worrying about the past and focus on the now.

Now, he had a new name.

Now, he ran a record store.

Thinking about the store led his thoughts back to Al Ferguson.

To stand up to Marlene Babb, the man threatened to unionize the store owners along the boardwalk. And he ended up dead.

He thought back to his conversation with the hipster.

The younger man had mentioned Al would kick him out of the store occasionally and pull the shades.

What was he doing inside where no one could see him?

***

When he couldn't take staring at the ceiling any longer, Owen flung the bedcovers back, got dressed, and returned to the boardwalk. It was almost two in the morning, and the bars would close soon.

As he passed Bart's Place, he saw the hipster inside. The younger man drank a dark-colored liquid and scanned the bar. When he noticed Owen, the hipster lifted his glass in salute.

Owen waved casually, then continued.

He was surprised how many people were out along the boardwalk at this time of night. It was crazy with activity.

Didn't these people have jobs?

Shouldn't they be in bed at this time of the morning?

He slowed as he considered those two thoughts.

Surely, he would never have cared when he was a Dawg. He was often out at this time of night. Their work—their *crimes*—were often committed under the veil of darkness. He also didn't care what others did, as long as it didn't affect him. His was a perspective of live and let live.

Now, he suddenly cared about what others did. Why?

It had to be his new perspective of civility built upon the concept of people living within society's boundaries. Once you step within those boundaries, your perspective changes—it *must* change. If it doesn't, you will be forced out. Society requires at least some conformity. Otherwise, it's anarchy.

He pressed on, passing his darkened shop.

Near the north end of the boardwalk, he came to Headbangers. The logo above the front door featured a giant guitar. Even with the lights turned off, it looked cool.

The big man glanced to his left and right before pulling on the front door. It was locked. He hadn't expected anything less. Overhead lamps still lit the boardwalk so anyone could see him. He didn't want to break in through the front door.

He slipped around the side of the building. Every structure stood so close as to allow passage only by turning sideways and shimming the length of the property line. When he popped out of the back, paint chips and debris had collected on his sweatshirt. He did his best to brush it off, but he was sure his back was covered as well.

The rear of the store abutted the alley. He could have walked down the alley from his house, but he wasn't sure exactly which building was Headbangers. Therefore, he had to come at it from the boardwalk.

Owen considered the back door. The building was of an age that it opened inward. He twisted the doorknob, hoping to find it unlocked. It remained firmly in place.

He then leaned his shoulder into the door, hoping to pop the lock. That didn't work. He then shoved his shoulder into the door. Again, no movement.

Pausing for a moment, he considered the front and rear doors. Neither showed evidence of forced entry. That meant, at least to Owen, that Big Al's killer must have known him. Of course, if the store was locked, why would Al have been inside? Wouldn't he have gone home?

Owen shook the thoughts free from his head. These considerations were better had indoors, away from prying eyes. He'd already been out here for a couple of minutes now. That was too long, and he should move on.

He glanced up and down the alley. There wasn't anyone moving, and the only people who could possibly see him were folks who lived in the houses. There was only one home with a light burning. A person with insomnia, perhaps? Or maybe they just left a light on.

The curtains remained closed, though, and none fluttered from movement.

He knew what he was about to do wasn't smart. The intelligent thing to do would be to keep his head down and let the police do their job. But Detective Roy Cochran was looking at him as a suspect. How long would it take a smart cop, which he truly believed the man to be, to find holes in his cover story? No matter how good the U.S. Marshals were, a seasoned detective would likely find something about Owen's backstory that didn't hold up to scrutiny. Then where would he be?

At his core, Owen was still a man of action, and doing something was better than waiting for the cops to show up on his doorstep. He'd instead try to clear his name and if he failed then let the police—well, he didn't want to think about that.

Owen took a deep breath and kicked the door. It popped open and banged against an interior wall. He stepped in and closed the door behind him.

Even though the store was dark, he knew better than to turn on the lights.

But as he moved deeper into the store, the illumination from the boardwalk lit up the shop. As his eyes adjusted to the low light, he took in Headbangers. On the walls and the shelves were mementos of thirty years of hard rock music.

Owen basked in the music and memorabilia of Al's life.

Posters of Metallica, Megadeth, Halestorm, Suicidal Tendencies, and more covered the walls. Autographed guitars hung on the walls. He looked at one red and white guitar and was sure Eddie Van Halen signed it. He covered his heart and smiled. But Owen wasn't there to reminisce. He wanted to know what Al Ferguson was up to.

As he turned away from the trinkets and knickknacks, a small flash of color caught his eye, and he stopped. He leaned toward a display rack and grabbed an Anthrax album. On the corner was a lime green price tag. Gritting his teeth, he was sure it was the same as those that Sam the Scavenger had brought him.

Owen tucked the album under his arm and proceeded through the store.

The hipster had said Al would kick everyone out of his store, lock the doors, and pull the shades.

What was he doing inside away from prying eyes?

The big man slowly walked through the store and looked for anything suspicious. He couldn't figure out any reason why Al would need to hide what was occurring inside.

Near the rear of the store, where he had entered, he found a door. Opening it led to a staircase up to an attic. Owen found a light switch and flicked it on. He quickly closed the door behind him to hide the light from anyone passing by on the boardwalk.

At the top of the stairs were boxes and other rock and roll displays. A tightly rolled sleeping bag sat on top of a cot. Owen considered it for a moment. Perhaps Al stayed there on late nights. Maybe he always slept in the shop. He wasn't sure it mattered, so he shrugged it off and continued deeper into the loft.

At its furthest part, near the front of the store, the attic had been cleared of debris and swept clean. A half-circle of chairs faced a map of the boardwalk hanging on the wall. Owen moved closer to inspect it. Every parcel and business were listed.

Colored in bright green was Headbangers.

Costa Buena Chillers, Seaside Surf Gear, and Grill, You Know It's True were colored green as well.

Bart's Place, The Babble, and Rockafellers, though, were each crossed out with a dark red X. The rest of the boardwalk was either unmarked or uncolored.

Owen stepped back from the map. Absently, he tapped the album in his hands while he thought. This was Al Ferguson's war room. Here was where he planned to organize the businesses against Marlene Babb. He spun around. There were only a few chairs and no printed materials. He put a hand on his hip and pursed his lips. He absently tapped the album against his leg while he continued to think.

Why was it so secret that he would kick out his customers?

Since the businesses were organizing against Marlene, they wouldn't want anyone to know. If Big Al closed the store and drew the shades, the attendees could enter through the alley and go directly into the attic. No one on the boardwalk would be any the wiser.

After the meeting, the attendees could leave and return to their respective stores. Al could lift the shades and return to business.

Owen tapped the map and considered Costa Buena Chillers and Seaside Surf Gear. He decided to visit them in the morning to find out what they talked with Al Ferguson about.

The first pieces of a puzzle were coming together, and he felt better after taking some action.

Owen hurried down the stairs, flicked off the light, and stepped into the quiet store. He stood still for several moments and listened. A group of people walked by on the boardwalk but didn't bother to investigate the darkened store.

He exhaled then. He hadn't realized he'd been holding his breath.

Quickly, he turned to the back door, pulled it open, and stepped outside. He was immediately blinded by a powerful light shining in his face.

"Freeze," a deep voice yelled. "Costa Buena Police. Get your hands up!"

Chapter 16

At night, the Costa Buena Police Department was like any small city police department. There were overworked officers, on-call detectives, and flickering fluorescent lights that wouldn't get addressed by the daytime staff who rarely used them.

Owen had been inside several departments like this before. However, he'd never been worried before. Tonight, however, he admitted to himself that he was more than slightly concerned. He had bigger things at stake than a burglary charge.

He was seated in an interview room, and his right hand was handcuffed to a steel railing bolted to the wall. His left hand lay on the table in front of him. His fingers tapped out a lazy rhythm despite what he felt inside.

On one wall of the room was a colorful poster with a scary shadow and headline that read, *See a Crime. Report it.* On the opposite wall was a bright sign with the cheerful banner, *Keep Costa Buena Bueno.*

"Detective Cochran is on his way," Officer Bragdon said. The lanky officer leaned against the far wall. He moved the toothpick into the corner of his mouth before speaking again. "He said he couldn't wait to talk with you."

Owen glanced up, nodded once, then returned to playing the lazy rhythm.

The officer, a tall man with red hair and freckles, watched Owen with curiosity. He pulled the toothpick from his mouth and pointed it at him. "Cochran doesn't mess around, ya know. He's the real deal."

The big man tapped his pinky finger several times, as if playing the piano. The rhythm he played was new, not something he'd heard before. He was riffing, making it up on the spot—anything to keep his mind from his worries.

"How'd you know I was in the store?" Owen asked.

"Concerned citizen called it in. Said they saw you kick the back door."

Owen had known better than to do it, but he still broke into the store. Before doing so, he even admonished himself for standing around in the alley. The caller was probably from the house with the light on.

"You should be worried," Bragdon said.

Owen nodded in time with the beat his fingers created.

The officer bent slightly to see Owen's eyes.

"Aren't you worried? We caught ya inside that store. With the door broken and all."

He looked up. "I have a right to remain silent, don't I?"

The officer's brow furrowed. "Sure."

"So do you."

Owen's tongue now clicked along with his fingers as they created the beat.

"Stop that clicking," the officer said.

His tongue became silent, but he continued his finger tapping. Officer Bragdon rolled his eyes.

This wasn't the first time Owen had been in an interview room. It wasn't even in the first dozen. To calm his nerves, he tried to assure himself that there was no reason to be concerned. But he knew there was.

He was a rat, living under the protection of the U.S. Marshals. Perhaps this might cause them to kick him out of the program. Or maybe they would violate his deal and send him to prison. Or maybe the Dawgs would get wind that he was in Costa Buena and hunt him down.

There were a lot of things to consider.

"What are you playing?" Bragdon asked.

"It's Morse Code."

Leaning in to listen, the officer asked, "Really?"

Owen couldn't do anything about his concerns while sitting in an interview room being watched by a freckle-faced officer. The best thing he could do right now was project a sense of peace, which is why he continued to tap his fingers.

He couldn't act scared around cops. At Headbangers, as long as he followed Bragdon's directions and remained silent, everything worked out fine. Well, as fine as could be expected.

"That's not Morse Code," the officer said with a smirk.

"Yes, it is."

"No, it's not. I used to be in the Army. I know Morse Code."

He paused his tapping. "It's pig Latin Morse Code."

"There's no such thing."

"How do you know? Pay attention now. See if you can follow along. I'll even slow it down."

The officer frowned and leaned in again. Owen resumed his tapping.

After arresting him, the officer ran his name through the criminal database and discovered Detective Cochran had flagged Owen. That meant anyone contacting Owen was to notify the detective. Cochran directed Officer Bragdon to hold him until he arrived.

All Owen could do now was wait for the detective to show up and interview him. Well, he'd try to talk with him. Owen would only share what he wanted. More than likely, though, he wouldn't tell Cochran anything.

As he tapped the table, he was already calculating what he would say. The best thing he could do was remain silent, and the law gave him that right. He intended to use it to the fullest.

In the end, Detective Cochran would no doubt get frustrated and book him for Burglary. They had him cold for that. But Owen knew Cochran didn't have any evidence to book him for the murder of Big Al Ferguson. He'd already told him that. Had Owen left well enough alone and not gone to Headbangers, he wouldn't be sitting in this room.

His tapping rhythm stumbled as he realized something.

"I almost had it," Bragdon said.

"What?"

"The code. Start again."

"Right," Owen said. "Sorry."

The officer's brow furrowed deeply in concentration.

It wasn't his first arrest, he thought, but it was Owen Hunter's. He wondered if a judge would go easy on him. That would be a change. No administrator of the law had ever gone easy on Beauregard Smith.

He hadn't expected to ever be in this situation again—handcuffed and in a police interview room. Owen wanted to turn around his life and be a better man.

The officer straightened, shaking his head. "That's not Morse Code, and that's not pig Latin."

Owen shrugged. "You got me."

"It's people like you," Bragdon said as he pointed his toothpick at the big man. "You move into our city and create all sorts of problems. You should have stayed where you were. We don't need you. We're doing fine all by ourselves."

Owen opened his mouth to speak, but there was a knock on the door.

Bragdon smiled. "Now, you're going to get yours."

When the officer opened the door, confusion crossed his face.

Standing in the doorway was a man in a dirty cowboy hat, a faded western shirt, blue jeans, and cowboy boots.

"Who are you?" Bragdon asked.

Holding an identification wallet at eye-level, the visitor said, "Special Agent Max Ekleberry. I'm here for Mr. Hunter."

"Sir?"

"See what this says?"

The officer leaned toward the wallet. "Federal Bureau of Investigation."

"Mr. Hunter is working a case with me."

"But he was arrested for—"

"For what?" Ekleberry challenged.

"Burglary," the officer muttered.

"Son, what I'm working on is so much higher up than burglary."

The officer glanced back at Owen.

"You ever stop to think—Look at me, son. You ever stop to think that maybe that burglary was part of what Mr. Hunter was working on?"

"How could I do that?" Bragdon asked. "I just found out he was working with you."

The agent shook his head. "I need to talk with him."

"You can't. I'm watching him."

Ekleberry glared at the officer.

"There's a detective—"

"A detective?"

"On his way to interview him."

"You called out a detective at night for a burglary?"

"No, sir. Your guy's a suspect in a murder."

Ekleberry's eyes moved to Owen, who shrugged in return.

"Well, son," the federal agent said, sizing up Officer Bragdon, "you better call someone so I can talk with my man. He's vital to a federal investigation affecting national security, and I don't want no surf-side detective messing it up."

Bragdon nodded. "Yes, sir. I'll be back."

The FBI man leaned into the hallway, his attention on the departing officer.

"What are you doing?" Owen whispered.

"Making sure he's gone. And..." Suddenly, Ekleberry stepped into the interview room. He dug out his car keys. Flipping through them, he located a handcuff key.

"Did you do it?" the agent asked, holding up the key.

"What are you doing?" Owen asked, jingling the handcuff around his wrist.

"Did you do it?" Ekleberry repeated.

"The burglary? Yeah, I did."

"No, ding-dong. The murder. Did you kill someone?"

"No, Max. I swear I didn't kill anyone."

He studied Owen's eyes for a brief moment before sticking the key into the cuff. With a quick twist, Owen was free.

"Let's go," the federal agent said, not bothering to see if the big man was on his heels. "We'll talk about this in my truck."

Chapter 17

"You created a mess, Beau."

"I didn't create this."

The lawman rolled his eyes.

"All right, I broke into the store, but I'm trying to find a killer."

"So, you're a cop now?"

"No," Owen said.

The big man leaned against the headrest. They were in Ekleberry's truck, headed toward the boardwalk.

"What made you do something stupid like breaking into a business?"

"I don't like being accused of murder."

The G-man snorted. "You've killed plenty of men in your time."

"That was before," Owen muttered. "Besides, they deserved it."

The lawman signaled a lane change. "Maybe you figured this guy deserved it."

"He was a citizen," the big man said. "I've never hurt a citizen. You know that."

They sped through an intersection as its light changed from yellow to red.

Ekleberry's eyes remained on the road when he said, "You and your code."

"Don't mock it."

"I'm not. It's the one thing that made me believe you still had some decency in you."

They drove in silence for a couple of minutes.

Owen faced the agent, whose face was pinched in concentration.

"How'd you find out about my arrest?"

"You're flagged."

"I know. Detective Cochran put me into the system."

"That's not what I'm talking about. Onderdonk put you in as well. Anytime something happens to you, I get notified. Whether it be your new name or your old one."

"Why?"

Ekleberry glanced toward Owen. "Because you're my responsibility, Beau."

They rode a couple of blocks in silence.

Staring ahead, the big man asked, "Why do you care?"

"I told you if you helped me, I would help you. You thought I was blowing sunshine, but I wasn't. I made you a promise, and I keep my promises."

"So, you got this alert and what, caught a flight out here? That was fast."

The agent chuckled. "I'm on vacation."

"In California? You drove here?"

"Lots of people drive to California for vacation."

"What were you doing?"

"A wine tour in the Napa Valley."

"By yourself?"

"My girlfriend is waiting for me to return. I left her to come help you."

"She can't be happy about that." Owen's eyes drifted to the agent's belt. "You bring your gun and badge on vacation?"

"When you were with the crew, did you stop being a Dawg if you ever took a break?"

"You're saying the FBI is a crew?"

"The biggest." A smile crossed Ekleberry's lips. "And the baddest."

"They're going to come for me."

"The detective?"

"And the police department."

"I'll call him," the lawman said. "What's his name?"

"Roy Cochran. Can you do me a couple of other favors?"

"Getting greedy, aren't you? I just saved you from going to jail—"

"Which I appreciate."

"—and you want more?"

"Run two names for me."

"This is a local crime. I shouldn't be involved."

"But it concerns my safety and well-being. Doesn't that make it federal?"

Owen pointed to his house, and Ekleberry pulled to a stop in front.

"What are the names?"

"Samuel Peyton. He's a local scavenger. Trades in albums and information."

The FBI man grabbed his notebook from the dashboard and jotted the name in it. "Got any descriptors? It's a fairly common name."

"Mid-fifties. Five and a half feet tall. Built like a bowling ball that rolled out of the sixties."

"And the other?"

"Marlene Babb."

"Who's she?"

"The local land baron."

When Ekleberry was finished writing, he glanced at Owen. "All right. I'll let you know what I find."

"By the way, where's Onderdonk? I called him yesterday and haven't heard back."

The lawman shrugged. "Maybe he's placing another witness. You know how Ted is. He'll get to you as soon as he can. He won't forget about you."

Owen nodded.

"Need anything else?"

"Just the names." He stuck out his hand, and the lawman took it. "Thanks, Max. I do appreciate your coming to my rescue."

"No problem, Beau. Don't make a habit of it."

Chapter 18

The ocean's breeze rushed in with her. She wore another smart suit—a brown jacket and skirt, tan blouse, and flats.

"We don't want your type in Costa Buena," she announced as she continued to march into the middle of the store.

"My type?"

Anita Moffett stamped her foot and held her fists by her side. "You know what I mean, Mr. Owen."

"I'm afraid I don't."

"You were arrested. For Burglary of Al Ferguson's business, no less."

"And?"

"And? *And?* That's enough, isn't it? That's a violation of a person's personal space. And the man just died."

"It's not what you think."

She stamped her foot again. "Then what is it?"

"I wanted to know why someone wanted to kill him."

Anita's eyes narrowed. "Why do you care?"

He couldn't tell her the real reason, so he said, "Because he sold records like me. Maybe I need to be worried that someone wants to kill me."

"That's a flimsy excuse," she said slowly.

"That's why I did it."

She crossed her arms and set her jaw. For a moment, she remained that way until saying, "I can't believe you're rationalizing what you did."

"I'm not rationalizing."

"You are."

Owen stared at her.

"You were also fighting," she said, her voice low and challenging.

"I didn't start that. Those punks came into—"

"Punks? That's disrespectful to the youth."

"Are you kidding me?" Owen muttered. "They aren't the youth. They're men. Gotta be close to thirty years old."

"The youth of today are different from the youth of yesterday."

"Now who's rationalizing? Those men destroyed property in my store *after* they tried to extort me."

"Do you have proof of that?"

He pointed to the little Elvis head on the counter. "That's all the proof you need—they broke the king of rock and roll."

She frowned. "You're not making sense."

"They broke my Elvis statue."

She picked up the Elvis head and examined it, looking at it from various angles.

"Those punks—"

Her eyes flared with anger, and he lifted his hands to calm her.

"I apologize," he said. "Those *misunderstood men* are bad news, and you refuse to see it."

"If that's true, if they really are bad news—"

Something fell in the back of the store, and she turned to look at it.

"The cat," he said.

"Cat Stevens."

"Nikki," he said with a mischievous smile.

She scowled. "If those men are really bad news, then you were the one who encouraged that behavior."

"Encouraged? How would I—? Why would I—? No, I never did. I never encouraged them. That bad behavior was already there."

She shook her head. "I'm not going to listen to this. I've decided to revoke your business license."

"You can't do that."

"I can, and I will."

"You're not with the government. You don't have the power."

"I'm the people," she said and stamped her foot. "That's all the power we need."

Her face was red, and her fists shook by her side.

Owen's eyes narrowed. "Who put you up to this?"

"What?" Her brow furrowed in confusion.

"You heard me."

"Nobody put me up to anything. I'm here because of the things you did. *You.* Nobody else."

"There's an old saying, and I'm sure you've heard it—follow the money."

"That's not an old saying."

"Old enough. If we follow the money, I'm betting it will lead back to Marlene Babb. She's part of your committee, isn't she? Some say she's your benefactor."

"Marlene isn't our—"

"How did you find out about my arrest last night?"

"What?"

"I'm barely home, and you're down here, busting my chops."

"Don't make this about me, Mr. Owen!"

"It's clearly about you."

"You are the one in the wrong. You are the bad element."

"I'm only trying to run a record store—."

"And doing a bang-up job of it." She spread her arms wide. "Full of customers."

Owen's eyes slanted.

Her face softened, and her arms dropped. "I'm sorry. That was mean and uncalled for."

"I think it's time you go."

"Mr. Owen," she said, her voice soft.

"It's fine," he said, pointing to the door, "but you need to go."

Anita pursed her lips. "You know I'm coming back, right?"

"I have no doubt."

She walked slowly to the door, opened it, glanced back once, then left.

Chapter 19

Owen studied the record in his hand. It was Def Leppard's second album, *High 'n' Dry*. On the cover was a picture of a man diving into an empty swimming pool. The photograph was superimposed over a crowd of men looking upward.

While not as big of a commercial hit as their third release, this album was loved by most fans of the band. These thoughts about album sales, fan considerations, and cover art were transitory, though. His true concerns were more detail oriented.

He slowly turned the album over, examining it from different angles. The cover was pristine—no cracks, wrinkles, or marks. Its original shrink wrap remained in place. The first owner presumably slit the plastic along the album's opening so they could carefully slide the record in and out. Someone took great care of this item.

Carefully, he pulled the black disk from the cover and its original slip. The record shone under the lights of the store. There wasn't a single scratch on either side. It was beautiful in its simplicity.

After putting the disk back inside the cover, Owen considered what had honestly bothered him all along—the green price sticker on the upper left corner of the front cover.

Had a thrift store employee in Rancho Chimera received this pristine album and slapped a sticker exactly resembling those from Owen's competitor? Or had Sam the Scavenger broken into Headbangers and stolen this album along with several crates of others?

His eyes slid over to Travis, who sat in the middle of the store licking himself.

"You know what I think?" The cat stopped and stared at him. "I think our friend has some questions to answer."

The door to the store opened, and Detective Roy Cochran stepped in. When his eyes landed on Owen, his upper lip curled. As the detective approached, the big man tucked the Def Leppard album into a nearby box, unconcerned that he was putting Def Leppard between The Falcons and The Flamingos.

The heavyset detective smirked as he ambled over. "Thought you would have been in the wind by now."

"Why's that?" Owen asked, moving behind the counter. He didn't want the detective noticing the boxes of albums with lime green stickers. He didn't want to tempt Cochran with a potential motive for murder.

"When a federal agent calls and says he's absconded with a suspected burglar from my interview room, well, I start to think something hinky is going on."

"Hinky?"

Cochran's tongue clucked against the roof of his mouth. "You must think I'm stupid."

"I don't think that."

"Me being a small-town detective and all."

"No, sir. I would never think that."

"I didn't start here."

Owen stared at him.

"I came from Chicago, where I ran across guys like you all the time."

He didn't like where this was headed. "Guys like me?"

"Guys that don't fit."

"How's that?"

"Something isn't right about you. You're too clean."

"What's that mean? Too clean?"

"The way you look. All tatted up. That face of yours."

Slightly offended, Owen touched his cheek. "What's wrong with my face?"

"You've got that look of having been in trouble, but your record says you're as fresh as a baby's bottom."

Not liking kids, Owen didn't appreciate the reference.

"There's not a scratch on your record," Cochran continued. "No pun intended."

"I'm not sure what to tell you," he muttered.

Owen wanted to fiddle with something to help hide his nervousness and searched for the little Elvis head. He'd left it on the counter, but now it was missing. He glanced toward the cat. Sensing Owen's displeasure, the tom bolted underneath a nearby stand.

"You've got some parking tickets and a couple speeding citations, but any real trouble? Oh, no. Not you, no, sir."

"Mama raised me right."

"See? There you go. Setting off my radar again."

Owen raised his hands and stepped back from the counter.

"You've got some important, connected friends."

"Agent Ekleberry, you mean."

"I did some checking on him. Know what he specializes in?"

Owen most certainly did, but he said, "Enlighten me," instead.

"Organized crime."

"Huh."

"That's all you got? *Huh?*"

"What do you want from me, Detective?"

"Organized crime makes a person think of the mafia."

"You think I'm in the mafia?" Owen asked.

"Not you. You're no goombah. Look at you. Too big, too tattooed, too heavy metal. If I didn't know better, I'd think you were in a band."

"Maybe I was. But I run a record store."

"You do now," Cochran said. Then repeated the words softer, as if thinking, "You do now."

"Listen, Detective. I broke into Big Al's store. I admit that. It was a bad decision. Your boys caught me fair and square."

"Fair and square?"

"I'll go before a judge—" Owen was hoping it would never come to that "—and plead my case, but I wanted to know what happened to Al."

"I told you what happened. He got hit over the head. End of story. There was no reason for you to go into that shop."

Cochran was smart. The detective was going to need a better reason than him just being curious.

"I wondered if you were telling the whole truth."

"So you committed a felony to see if I, an officer of the law, told the truth? Your decision-making is suspect."

"Some of us on the boardwalk are worried."

"What would you and the others have to worry about?" Cochran spoke slowly as his eyes searched Owen's.

The big man had scored with the last revelation. He needed to continue working that point to give the detective a new rabbit to chase.

"The businesses were organizing against their landlord."

Cochran relaxed. "Their landlord?" he said, shaking his head. "You mean Marlene Babb?"

"She's got them scared."

"The woman's a saint."

"Of course she is."

"You can't be implying that a group of business owners were afraid of a sweet ol' gal like her. You're grasping at straws, Mr. Hunter."

"I'm telling you the truth. She's—"

The detective held up a hand, cutting him off. "Marlene puts on an annual fundraising barbecue for the department. Big spread down on the beach. Ribs, chicken, potato salad." Cochran's eyes took on a misty gleam. "There's usually so much food we all take a platter home. Good for a couple more meals. The lady's a civic gem."

Owen shoved his hands into his pockets. "A gem?"

Cochran refocused. "Doesn't make any sense that the businesses would be pushing back against her."

"I should talk with someone else. You seem to be sweet on Marlene."

"I'm not sweet on her. She's pushing seventy-five."

"You're sweet on her barbecue then."

The detective shrugged. "Probably, but that doesn't mean I can't put the job first."

Owen considered the cop. He found him to be a reasonably competent law enforcement officer. But the allegiance to Marlene Babb was disturbing.

"Tell me what you know, Mr. Hunter."

"Marlene owns all the property along the boardwalk. She's raising rents, not taking care of broken items."

"*All* the property? I didn't know that."

"All the properties except this one." Owen pointed to the ground.

"And she wants it?"

He nodded.

The detective glanced up at the pictures on the wall. "How'd you get it?"

"I bought it from the estate of Prescott Honeywell."

"But you're not from around here. How did you know it was available?"

"My attorney," Owen said. "He let me know."

Cochran's eyes dropped down to the big man. "Your attorney? You got an attorney looking for a property for you to invest in?"

Owen gnawed on the inside of his lip as he thought. He'd said too much, and the detective knew it. There was a change in the room's energy as the detective's head tilted slightly to the side, and his eyes narrowed.

"Who's your attorney?"

"Excuse me?" As soon as Owen said it, he regretted it.

Cochran smiled. His question had scored a bullseye. "Your attorney. What's his name?"

"Why?"

"To confirm your story."

"Let me talk with him first."

The detective's smile grew larger. "To get your facts straight? You know you never did tell me how you acquired this business so quick after Prescott Honeywell's death."

"Why's that matter?"

"Doesn't smell right."

Owen folded his arms.

"If you killed Al Ferguson, your federal agent friend can't protect you."

"I didn't kill him."

"But you broke into his store."

"I already admitted that."

"We caught you inside there. It doesn't matter if you admit it or not."

"But I told you why I did it. I wanted to know if any of the other business owners on the boardwalk are in danger."

Cochran rubbed his face as he thought. When he came to a decision, he clicked his tongue against the back of his teeth. "You think we're small time, Mr. Hunter—"

"No, I don't."

"—and that's okay because we are. It's one of the reasons I moved out here. But because of my experience and training, I know how to use the resources afforded me."

"Which means?"

"I've called for outside help."

"Outside help?"

"The California Bureau of Investigation."

Owen swallowed.

"That's right, hotshot. You may have a federal agent in your corner. But I'm bringing in my own suits. I'm going to figure out what's going on with you, who you are, and what you're hiding. And when I do, we'll have a different conversation then."

Cochran strode toward the door. As he did, he passed Travis peering out from underneath a table.

"Hey, Possum," he muttered, then yanked the front door open and disappeared down the boardwalk.

Chapter 20

"Was that a cop?"

Owen's head snapped back to the door.

U.S. Marshal Theodore "Ted" Onderdonk stood in the doorway. He wore a short-sleeved plaid shirt, khaki pants, and brown loafers. The wear marks showed on his leather belt from where his badge and gun should have been.

Owen's head dropped, and he dejectedly shook it. "Yeah," he said. "Local detective."

The lawman glanced back down the boardwalk before quietly closing the door. "What's he doing here?"

"I was arrested last night."

"I got the alert. I was surprised to learn you got out."

"You haven't talked to Ekleberry then?"

"Max is involved?"

"He's out here on vacation. He got the same alert you did."

Onderdonk glanced out the window toward the ocean. "He's in California?"

"He's in wine country with his girlfriend."

"Is he still mad about what happened in Maine?"

"He seems to have gotten over it."

The lawman raised his eyebrows.

"You should still call the man and apologize." Owen couldn't believe he was giving relationship advice to the two lawmen responsible for pulling him out of the Satan's Dawgs and slapping him into the Witness Protection Program.

"After I deal with whatever you got yourself into," Onderdonk said, half-heartedly. "So tell me, Beau, what did you do?"

"I broke into a business."

"A business?"

"Down the street."

"What the heck did you do that for?" The marshal tossed his hands in the air, then turned away in frustration. "What part of don't develop habits from your old life did you not understand?"

"The shop owner was murdered and—"

"Wait," the lawman said, turned quickly toward him. "You didn't—"

"No, Ted—"

"Because if you killed a man in cold blood, I can't protect you."

"I didn't kill any—"

"I thought the California sun and sand would be good for you."

"Listen to me."

"I am."

"I didn't kill anyone. Someone else did it, but the cops suspect me. Sort of."

"Sort of?"

"I think they were leaning toward not suspecting me..."

"Then you broke into the dead man's business and got them all riled up again."

Owen shoved his hands into his pockets and set his jaw.

"Why did they initially suspect you?"

"Because the business owner and I had a dust-up."

"You've only been here for three days."

"Happened on the first day."

Onderdonk rolled his head around his shoulders, eliciting several loud pops. "Can't you play nice with others?"

"I was trying."

"What caused the dust-up?"

Owen thumbed toward the poster hanging on the wall behind the counter.

The marshal tilted his head. "Mötley Crüe? This is an oldies shop."

"The Crüe *is* oldies. They came out over thirty-five years ago."

Onderdonk put his hands on his hips. "Good Lord. Those guys are that old now?"

"That's what I'm saying. And the guy who owned Headbangers—"

"The other shop?"

"Right. Big Al was spitting nails about me wanting to sell music past sixty-five."

"Sixty-five?"

"Your boy Prescott made a deal that this store wouldn't sell any music newer than nineteen sixty-five."

"Didn't leave you much to work with," Onderdonk said.

"That was my argument. So Big Al and I had words, and he punched me. Later that night, he was murdered. The cops suspect me."

The marshal stepped forward and leaned on the counter. "They're local cops. They like things nice and simple. By breaking into his store, you handed them a murder suspect on a silver platter.”

“I know.”

“That’s the worst thing you could do.”

“*I know.*”

“No, you don’t, or you wouldn’t have done it. You don’t understand a cop’s mind.”

“I think I do.”

“You’re wrong. You might have understood how they thought about the *old* you, the criminal version of you, Beauregard Smith. But the new you, Owen Hunter, he’s going to be an enigma to them.”

“An enigma?”

“A puzzle covered by government-funded secrets and lies. You don’t think a cop like this... what’s his name?”

“Roy Cochran.”

“You don’t think this Roy Cochran is going to want to solve a puzzle of this magnitude just to do it? That’s like giving a Rubik’s Cube to some brainiac. He’s going to work it until it’s solved.”

Owen swallowed. Roy’s threat of the California Bureau of Investigation immediately came back to him.

“Why did you think breaking into the other store was a good idea?”

“He was doing something secretive in there.”

“You risked a lot going in there, so I hope you found something.”

"I did," Owen said. "The boardwalk businesses were unionizing against the local land baron."

"Is that a thing? The unionizing of businesses. Can they do that?"

"I don't think they can unionize, but the murder victim was definitely organizing them."

"Like a crew."

"Like a crew," Owen said, thinking about the Satan's Dawgs.

Onderdonk tapped the counter as he thought. Finally, he said, "So, this Detective Cochran thinks you killed the shop owner?"

"He suspects, yeah."

"Because of an argument in your store? How did he find out about that?"

"There was a witness to it. He told Cochran I threatened Big Al."

"Did you?"

"Not really."

Onderdonk threw his hands in the air once more. "What the heck does that mean?"

"The guy punched me, Ted. I didn't hit him back. I just muttered some words after he left."

The marshal squinted. "What words?"

"I owe you one."

"I owe you," Onderdonk repeated. "Low profile, Beau. *Low profile.* That's what I said, right?"

"That's what you said."

The lawman shook his head while he thought.

Travis strolled out from under a display table to stare at the marshal. Onderdonk knelt to pet the tom. "You never said thank you."

"For what?"

"For saving your cat."

"That's not my cat."

The cat licked its paw.

"He seems comfortable around you."

"It should have stayed with the bookstore," Owen said. "It's a bookstore cat."

"I can take him with me if you don't want him."

He eyed the cat as Onderdonk ran his hand from head to tail. "It's all right, I guess. Keeps the mice away. Good for protecting the records."

When the marshal stood, there were several pops in his knees. "This is messed up."

"Tell me about it."

"You're not in imminent danger."

"What's that mean?"

"I can't take this to my supervisor and request a move."

"I'm not asking for one. At least, not yet."

Onderdonk continued as if he didn't hear Owen. "She'll ask if you did it and you know what I'll have to say? I'll have to say, 'He told me he didn't do it.' She'll look at me like I lost my mind."

Owen crossed his arms. "I'm not asking to be moved."

"She'll also remind me that you're a killer."

"Not anymore."

"You killed that mob boss back in Pleasant Valley."

"He threatened to kill someone I cared for."

"What about the guy who washed up on the shore in a neighboring town? You wouldn't know anything about him, would you?"

Owen shrugged. He did know how the body ended up there, but now wasn't the time nor the place for that discussion.

"Your track record alone is reason enough for me to stand back and see what local PD finds on this."

"I'm not asking for a move, Ted, but I'm not feeling a lot of loyalty, either."

"Maybe I could get a contingency plan in place. Maybe I could sell my boss on that. Do you feel like you are in imminent danger?"

"Roy Cochran," Owen said. "He's looking deeper into my background because he says I'm too clean."

"Too clean?"

"He said someone who looks like me should have more on their record than some vehicle-related citations. That's profiling."

"Criminal profiling," Onderdonk said with a frown.

"Whatever. He's calling the California Bureau of Investigations to help. Is that even a thing?"

"It is, for sure." The marshal rubbed his chin while he thought. "I can work with this. I'll monitor what they're doing. If they get too close to your real identity, I'll have the authority to pull you out and relocate you."

Owen watched the lawman as he worked out the problem in his head.

"But I would say this," the marshal said, "if you can prove you're innocent in any way, do it. Don't wait around for the local cops to point the crooked finger of justice at you."

"The crooked finger of justice?"

"It still points in the right direction, doesn't it?"

"Funny how that works."

Onderdonk hooked his thumbs into his pockets. "This is a mess, Beau."

"You said that already."

"What else can I do to help? Without relocating you, of course."

"Tell me about Prescott."

The lawman raised an eyebrow. "Honeywell? What about him?"

"How'd he end up here? I feel I need to know something about him if I'm going to prove my innocence."

Onderdonk thought about the request for a moment, then nodded. He wandered over to the front door, flipped the *Open* sign to *Closed*, and spun the lock, securing the door.

"You're going to like this story."

Chapter 21

"Prescott Honeywell?" Owen said. "Sounds like a fancy pants. I thought cover names in the WitSec program were supposed to be boring."

"Not all of them."

"Mine is."

"Owen Hunter is not boring."

"Owen is totally boring."

"It's a fine name."

"For a nerd."

"Quit being a baby," the lawman said. He leaned an elbow on the counter. "If you ever met the man, you'd understand why he earned the name. He was a regular fussbudget."

"What did he do?"

"He was a scam artist."

"A grifter?"

"That's like lumping Picasso in with a house painter. Mozart in with..." Onderdonk's eyes drifted to the poster on the wall, "Mötley Crüe."

"I like the Crüe."

"And I like Pabst Blue Ribbon. That doesn't make me a beer connoisseur."

Owen smirked.

"Prescott's real name was Alexander Zacharia Swoboda."

"Alphabet soup."

"His mother oversaw the games of chance for a traveling carnival. They plied their trade through the rust belt. His father ran an illegal poker game that followed the circus. Guess who made more money?"

"Mom?"

"Of course. Unsuspecting marks walk up and gladly hand over their hard-earned dollars in exchange for an out-weighted opportunity to win a cheap prize. It was a sheer numbers game. There are far more people willing to lose five or ten dollars than there are willing to play poker and lose hundreds. Mama Swoboda raked in the money hand over fist."

The cat moved to the lawman and rubbed against his leg.

Owen sat on the stool behind the counter. "The man grew up in a circus but was a fussbudget?"

"When chaos is your world, you rebel by going straight."

"I didn't," Owen said.

"Stop interrupting," Onderdonk said. "So young Alexander internalized his mother's teachings, and from his father, he learned how to count cards. Then he did what any enterprising young man would do."

"He went to Vegas."

"He went to college. I told you he went straight. Keep up."

Owen frowned.

"But while in school, Alexander ran a side business."

"Poker games?"

The lawman tapped his nose.

"So, he wasn't entirely straight?"

"Straight enough. You see, he didn't play poker. He'd learned from his father's mistakes. Instead, he ran a poker room inside his apartment, always taking a percentage from the players who were there. He took a few dollars for entry, then he'd take a small fee every hour to cater to the guys playing in the games."

"Where did the scam come in?"

"Who said there was a scam?

"You said he was a scam artist."

"Hold your horses. Right now, he's going to school. Learning things. He's charging a fee to run the games and enjoying the life of a college student. The kid had the tiger by the tail, so to speak. Then one day, a local mobster in the Philadelphia area walks in. Donny Fingers—"

"Named because...?"

"He was pinched for shoplifting while a kid. Anyway, Donny says the kid can't be running illegal card games in his town without paying tribute to the crew."

Owen smiled. "College hadn't taught him the right things."

"Alexander wasn't stupid and agreed to pay Donny's family. He kicked up the twenty percent that Donny wanted. Knowing the mob was looking out for him and that they wanted him to be successful, Alexander expanded. Soon, he had illegal card rooms in several apartments. He'd bounce from apartment to apartment throughout the night, checking on the players, making sure they got what they needed. He even hired girls to provide them drinks."

"Girls?"

Onderdonk nodded. "The college kids loved them. The percentage Alexander was kicking up got so big that Donny Fingers grew jealous. He realized how much he had to be making for himself, so he moved in and pushed the kid out. Took over the whole darn thing. With Alexander out, though, the college kids stopped coming. They didn't want to play cards with a mobster standing over their shoulder.

"Donny hadn't thought about that before letting his greed get the better of him. The bosses were none too happy that their easy income stream suddenly dried up. Donny was in Dutch for overstepping his bounds. He was instructed to bring the kid back and let him run the games as he saw fit."

Owen shifted on his stool. "That had to make Donny very unhappy."

"You would think, as he was being told to listen to some snot-nosed college kid, right? So he went to Alexander, hat in hand, and told him to take over the games again. But the kid saw the writing on the wall. He probably would never have seen it if it weren't for Donny pushing him out."

The lawman paused as if waiting for Owen to interrupt, but the big man sat quietly with his brow furrowed in concentration.

Onderdonk continued. "Alexander realized the games only had a shelf life of a couple more years since he would soon age out of the college scene. When that happened, they would need to bring in someone else or shut the whole thing down. Therefore, he agreed to take over the games on one condition—after he got his accounting degree, he could slide into a better position within the mob."

Owen nodded. "He was going to school for an education—"

"But life gave him a better one. So Donny took Alexander's request to Johnny Seagull, the—"

"Johnny Seagull?"

"Terrible nickname, huh? Remember Jonathan Livingston Seagull? That touchy-feely book from the seventies?"

"No."

"Not a reader. I forgot. Anyway, the book was super popular in the early seventies when everybody was searching for themselves or some such nonsense. Anyway, Johnny Seagull got caught reading it, and the goombahs nailed him with that nickname. Stuck with him until the end."

"Horrible," Owen said. "No respect from this crew."

"Johnny Seagull oversaw the entire Philly crew by the early eighties. He liked what Alexander was doing. Appreciated the kid's smarts and his ambition. He agreed to bring in the youngster and make him an accountant if the kid would give a bigger cut of the college poker games over the next couple of years. Alexander did. He ran the poker circuit for a few more years then slid into the role of a mob accountant.”

Owen straightened. “Wait. You said he was a scam artist, but I still haven’t seen the scam yet.”

The lawman stared at him, waiting for him to catch up. Owen paused and replayed the conversation in his head.

Alexander goes to college and begins hosting poker games. Donny Fingers shows up and demands a cut. After a bit, Fingers takes over the games, which closes them down. When Donny Fingers is forced to ask Alexander to restart them, the kid explains the games only have a shelf life of another couple years. Then he tells them that he’s getting a college degree and wants to be an accountant for the mob. That’s when Johnny Seagull agrees to the deal. He runs the games for a couple more years then moves into a full-time position with the mob.

Owen rubbed his head as he considered the scenario.

Where is the scam?

He couldn’t see it unless it started from the very beginning. The big man’s eyes slowly returned to the marshal. “He wasn’t going to school to be an accountant, was he?”

“You’re smarter than you look.”

“What was he doing?”

“At that point, he hadn’t decided. He was only getting his general requirements out of the way. But when Donny Fingers opened the door, Alexander knew what he needed to run the biggest scam of all, so he started his accounting degree."

"While running the poker games?"

"Graduated at the top of his class."

"Where's the scam in that?"

"There was none," Onderdonk said. "Yet. But as soon as he was inside, Alexander worked with an elderly accountant. The guy knew where all the money was hidden and knew how all the books were cooked. The old man had a heart condition, and the crew needed to get someone up to speed and fast. Who better than a young, enterprising man who wanted to grow with the mob?"

"Here it comes," Owen said, leaning toward the marshal.

"Alexander paid attention, listened, and learned. He discovered how the system worked, how there was another accountant from another crew who always audited his work. He reviewed their work as well. It was a lot to learn, but Alexander took it all in. Johnny Seagull was incredibly impressed with the young man's work ethic. He was the perfect employee. Then, about a year after he started, the old man passed away, which left Alexander to handle the books alone.

"Every day, he went to work, pretended to be a loyal accountant, then searched for an angle to get at all the money. He was trying to out-crook the crooks, trying to out-thieve the thieves.

"What he failed to realize early on was they were the masters of corruption. They had everyone watching everyone else. It was like the inside of a casino. There was an unhealthy level of paranoia and distrust surrounding their money.

"He invested his youth into learning a skill to get at the money. His mother and father passed while he fought with those windmills. He never had a girlfriend during that time—only the occasional lover to provide a cover for his constant quest to get at the money. He spent so much time attempting to steal something, but it always remained a little out of reach. He couldn't get it, couldn't have it. In the end, the money haunted him."

Owen nodded, taking it all in. "The whole thing had to make him crazy."

"The anticipation, the frustration, the anger—all of it caused Alexander to question if he was on the right path." Onderdonk glanced back out the window. "No matter what he did, no matter what plans he made, none of them got him closer to the money. It finally dawned on him that he couldn't steal it. Not without everyone knowing he was the one who took it. If even one dime came up missing, the entire Philly mob would know it. No matter what else he thought, he knew he wasn't going to be able to get it away without everyone knowing he was the person behind the theft. The mob would chase him forever."

The lawman turned back to Owen. "So, what would you do?"

"I don't know."

"Would you give up, put your head down, and accept your lot in life as a mob accountant?"

"Probably not."

"Or would you walk away and start life anew, hiding out forever, since what you knew was likely to get you killed?"

Owen shrugged. "Doesn't sound like a great alternative for all that time and effort invested."

"Or would you transfer every last dime to yourself, then run out the front door, knowing full well you were now a wanted man?"

The big man smirked. "You call that a scam artist?"

"That wouldn't be much of a scam, would it?"

"So, what happened?"

The marshal lifted his eyebrows a couple of times before continuing his story. "Alexander Zacharia Swoboda strolled into the offices of the FBI the next morning with an offer. In exchange for what he knew, he would get a new life, and he'd be allowed to keep ten percent of the money he reported. He would show them, to the penny, exactly where the Philadelphia crew hid all their money and their assets."

Owen's mouth slowly dropped open. "And the government agreed?"

"Alexander knew how to play the game of poker successfully. You never sit at the table. Instead, you only take a taste of the game that the real players are engaged in. Of course, the FBI agreed."

Chapter 22

Owen stared down at the sales counter. After listening to Marshal Onderdonk's story, he had to admit he admired the ingenuity and guts Alexander Swoboda displayed in ripping off the mob. The man might not have gotten everything he wanted, but Alexander bought himself a new life and extra time in the Witness Protection Program, plus he got to keep some of the cash he'd stolen.

Then Owen realized Alexander's alter-ego, Prescott Honeywell, did something else along the same lines. He looked up and said, "Prescott made a deal to sell the building."

The lawman's eyes drifted to the ceiling. "It wasn't his to sell."

"Was it in his name?"

"It was made to look that way—like it was a company he owned. However, the incorporation documents give him no power to sell or transfer the property. Those documents are not public records. We did the same thing for you."

"I don't remember signing anything like that."

The marshal smiled. "You didn't, but Owen Hunter did."

Owen tilted his head.

"Relax, it's part of your cover. Who was Prescott supposedly selling the building to?"

"Marlene Babb."

"Is she wrapped up in your troubles?"

"I think so. She's the local land baron and owns every building along the boardwalk except this one."

"Wow."

"I know. And she's an Ebenezer Scrooge type. Raising rents, not fixing anything. At least, that's what I've been told. The businesses on the boardwalk were beginning to organize against her."

"That's interesting."

"According to a local, Prescott agreed to sell the building to her if he ever left Costa Buena."

Onderdonk's brow furrowed. "Or he died?"

"Exactly. The talk was he was a pretty good surfer."

"He was, I think."

"If someone killed him," Owen said, "could they have made it look like an accident?"

"A staged surfing accident? I don't think so. Besides, I've read the coroner's report. He had water in his lungs. Pretty hard to fake that."

"Huh."

"Do the cops know about the agreement between Prescott and Marlene?"

"Not that I know of. And if they do, they're not doing anything about it. Marlene's a big donor to the department. Besides, she hasn't come forward to challenge my ownership of the building. She's playing it close to the vest. Even trying to get me to sell it to her now."

The lawman scratched the side of his face. "You said Ekleberry knows about this. What's he doing?"

"He's looking into Marlene."

Onderdonk's brow furrowed. "While he's on vacation?"

The big man shrugged. "He said he'd get back to me as soon as possible."

"I'll poke around, too. See what I can find."

Owen nodded. "I'd appreciate it. I don't enjoy the idea of going back to prison. Especially for something I didn't do."

The marshal tapped the counter. "Stay out of trouble, Beau."

"Hey, Ted."

"Yeah?"

"Have you heard from... her?"

"Who?"

"Daphne. The girl in—"

"No," Onderdonk flatly said.

Owen's shoulders dropped slightly.

The lawman pointed a finger at him. "Let her go." His voice was stern. "Don't even think about her. Doing so will lead you to do something stupid that will come back to haunt you."

His chest tightened.

"Be smart about this and forget her." Onderdonk headed for the door. He stopped with his hand on the doorknob and turned back to Owen. "Witness protection is about the long game. It's not about your feelings."

When he was alone, Owen stood in the middle of the store with his hands on his hips. He took in a deep breath and sighed.

Travis rubbed against his leg.

"Yeah," he said, "I miss her, too."

Chapter 23

Owen stood outside Costa Buena Chillers with his hand on the door. He looked through the window at the commotion inside.

For a weekday afternoon, the place resembled a war zone. Screaming children ran rampant through the small establishment as beleaguered and bewildered parents looked helplessly on. In their tiny hands, each child held an impossibly large colorful drink. Every shade of the rainbow was represented.

Behind the counter stood a mid-forties woman. She watched the activity with the dull eyes of a prison guard.

With his lip curling, he released the door's handle and stepped back. The big man didn't want to go in there. He disliked children. For that matter, he disliked the parents of children, too.

But he wanted—no, he *needed*—to talk with the owner of Costa Buena Chillers. He could wait for the business to slow, but when that might occur, he had no idea.

Besides, he was once the feared bookkeeper for the Satan's Dawgs. Why was he letting a store full of ankle-biters worry him? He should march in there, ignore the screaming and commotion of the little heathens, and just talk with the store's owner. He had a mission, and nothing should stop him from achieving it.

Owen grabbed the handle but again froze.

Even Superman had kryptonite, right? It was something innocuous to everyone else, but it was deadly to The Man of Steel. Children were Owen's kryptonite—the thing that made him weak with fear.

A pit grew in his stomach, and he fought back his dread. He needed to face these fears. He had to run a gauntlet of those smelly little urchins and their dreadful parents to get the information he required.

It was now or never.

With a yank, he opened the door.

The screams and giggles of little children flooded out of Costa Buena Chillers. Owen stepped in, and the door closed behind him. As it secured, the noise level increased. He felt slightly queasy.

Owen marched through the store, his eyes straight ahead. He refused to notice the glances from the harried mothers. He sidestepped dancing children and grimaced when a toddler squealed with delight.

At the counter, he stood behind a flustered father who held the hand of a bouncing young boy.

"Berry Berry Melon Blast!" the kid exclaimed, jumping higher each time.

"Say please," the father said, struggling to keep his voice calm.

"Berry Berry Melon Blast!" the boy repeated now, hopping quicker than before.

Behind the counter, the woman with the bored eyes turned to the chiller machine.

The father lowered himself until his face was level with his son's. "Norman," he pleaded, "please say *please*."

"Berry Berry Melon Blast!" The boy rocketed up and down, his hands clapping above his head with every jump.

The big man glanced over his shoulder at the rest of the other children. They were all now chanting "Berry Berry Melon Blast" in time with the jumping boy.

Several rattled mothers admonished their children to "Stop it!" with no measurable effect. The children in the store rocked back and forth, each clutching a large, colorful drink in their little hands. Oblivious to parental controls while in the throes of a sugar high, the kids gleefully chanted like a mob.

Owen smirked at the pint-sized riot, then turned back toward the counter.

"Please, Norman," the father begged, pointing to the clerk. "Say *please* to the lady."

"Berry Berry Melon Blast!" the kid hollered again, his hands clapping front-to-back now as he danced a jig.

The clerk politely smiled as she handed the boy an overly large, red, frozen drink.

The father shrugged and said, "I'm sorry," to the woman.

"I understand," she slowly said before announcing the price of the drink.

As the father paid, Norman jumped and continued his chant. The rest of the children joined in his celebration of the icy concoction.

In a moment of wild abandonment, the boy spun rapidly, raising and lowering his drink.

"Watch it—" Owen growled, but the warning came too late.

As the little boy's hands and arms were extended to full height in reverence to the supreme sugary goodness that surely awaited him, Norman collided with Owen.

The lid popped off, the base of the clear plastic cup quickly collapsed, and the red contents exploded over the big man's T-shirt and jeans before cascading down to his Converse.

"Berry Berry Melon Blast!" Norman screamed.

The other children squealed in delight as the frozen blend splattered to the tile floor.

"My drink!" the boy shrieked and pointed an accusatory finger at Owen. "My drink!"

The father stared at the bigger man.

Owen expected him to apologize or perhaps offer to pay for the cleaning of his clothes.

Instead, a sadness crossed over the man's face. It was a look he had seen before when doing the work of a Satan's Dawg bookkeeper. It was the melancholy a man experiences right before his death. Owen took this to mean only one thing—the father was silently imploring him to kill him and save him from the further misery of long lines at the side of a bratty child.

But it turned out he had read the signals wrong.

Owen watched as the father slowly turned to the bored-eyed clerk and asked, "Can we get another Berry Berry Melon Blast?"

***

In the backroom of Costa Buena Chillers, Owen used a wet washcloth to wipe most of the red liquid from his clothing and shoes. It would stain everything, no doubt, but he wanted to get the remaining frozen chunks off himself.

"I'm sorry about that," Lily Brummett said.

Lily owned the business and introduced herself after the unfortunate accident. "It happens more than you think."

"How do you stand it?"

"What?"

He jerked his head toward the roomful of kids. "Working with them and those... *parents*. All that squealing."

Lily forced a smile, but it conflicted with the dullness in her eyes. "It's not so bad once you get used to it."

"That's like saying a root canal isn't bad once you get used to it."

"What can I do for you, Mr. Hunter?"

"Owen," he said, tossing the now red washcloth into the sink. "Let's talk about Al Ferguson."

Her face flattened, and the fake smile disappeared. Suspicion replaced the boredom in her eyes. "What about Al?"

"You were organizing against Marlene Babb."

Lily moved toward the door to the lobby. "I'm sorry about what happened out there, but I think it's time for you to go."

"I'm not trying to cause you trouble."

She leaned in and whispered, "I don't know you, Mr. Hunter. As far as I know, you could be working for her."

"I'm not."

Lily glanced toward the front, then returned her focus to him. "Two people I knew on this boardwalk are dead. I don't want to get involved."

"The cops think I killed Al."

She folded her arms, and her eyes narrowed. "Did you?"

"If I did, why would I be here?"

"Trying to throw them off the scent. People do it all the time in the movies."

"That's not me. I'm not that smart."

"A smart person would say that. Again, trying to throw the cops off the scent."

Owen shook his head. "Lily, you don't know me. I don't know you. All I'm trying to do is find out who killed Al and why."

"And you're doing this because? Out of the goodness of your heart?"

"I need to prove my innocence before the cops railroad me."

She pursed her lips as she thought.

He figured changing the topic might get her to open up. "Prescott Honeywell was supposed to be a pretty good surfer."

Her face relaxed, and she shrugged. "He was. I'd see him out there. How he made money in his shop, I'll never know. The guy always closed it to go out and surf. It was like he didn't care."

Owen nodded in understanding. Prescott wouldn't care. The marshals would make sure the business was profitable, or at least Prescott didn't starve to death. And besides, if he kept ten percent of the money that he stole from the Philly mob, he would have been set financially enough to surf whenever he wanted.

"They say he drowned," Owen said.

"That's what they say."

"You think something else could have happened?"

"All I know is Prescott didn't want to sell his business to Marlene Babb, and he ended up dead. I didn't think much of it when it happened. I mean, it was sad, and all, but accidents happen, especially on the water. Then Big Al gets murdered. Two guys dead. Both on the wrong side of that woman. You know what they say—where there's smoke, there's fire."

The big man rubbed his chin.

"If you're trying to solve Al's murder, you need to look into her and her nephew."

"Nephew?"

Lily nodded. "He moved in a while back to help her out. Supposedly, he's some sort of problem solver. At least, that's what he says."

"A problem solver?"

"Yeah. He loves to say how he's here to manage situations—"

Manage situations, Owen thought.

"But what he's really doing is anybody's guess. He likes to pretend he's running Bart's Place."

"What's his name?"

"Titus Forsberg. You can't miss him. He's always dressed like some reject from a computer club."

Chapter 24

"For real, Honey Bear could cut waves like nobody's business. I wouldn't lie about that."

Owen had stopped into Seaside Surf Gear to continue his investigation.

Geoff Pemberton's long gray hair hid his face as he bent over a surfboard, slowly dragging a bar of wax back and forth. He wore an opened Hawaiian shirt over a hooded sweatshirt—a man refusing to relinquish the summer back to the incoming cooler weather. He also wore board shorts and flip-flops.

"Honey Bear?"

"Some of the beach Betties nicknamed him that. Sort of cute, right?"

Geoff lifted his head and flicked his hair back. The smell of marijuana and patchouli oil emanated from him. His smile was crooked, and his blue eyes were unfocused. He blinked several times before glancing up and down at Owen's clothing.

"You kill something, man?"

"I spilled my drink."

Geoff's face pinched. "Musta been a big one."

"It was. Did he have a girlfriend?"

"Occasionally," Geoff shrugged, "but a lot less than the average dude. Seemed like he didn't care too much. Know what I mean? I think he was more interested in surfing and listening to music than chasing the ladies and making money." Geoff stared off into the distance. "Whoa. Life philosophy. You think maybe he figured it right?"

Owen shrugged. "I don't know."

"I mean, I got lady problems. All sorts, you know?"

"Sure."

Geoff chuckled. "Maybe ol' Honey Bear had it right. Ditch the ladies. Stop worrying about the business. Just listen to music and surf." He paused to swoosh his hand, holding it dramatically out in front of him and staring at it. "Maybe if we all did that, everything would take care of itself. What do you think?"

Owen smirked. He never went for the ramblings of a stoned man. When guys in the Dawgs got high, it irritated him that they thought they solved the world's problems by toking on a joint. "It would be hard to eat tunes and waves."

"Yeah," Geoff said, his eyes drifting down his surfboard. "And no ladies. I don't even want to comprehend that. I mean, that sounds terrible. It's the whole reason I got into surfing."

"There you go."

"My girlfriend would be mad if I stopped working."

"You gotta do what you gotta do," Owen muttered. He was thinking that conversing with the stoned-out Geoff Pemberton was a waste of his time. He glanced over his shoulder. Maybe he could take off and head down the boardwalk. He wanted to find the hipster now and ask him about his relationship with Marlene Babb.

"I couldn't do that to her," Geoff said.

"Do what?"

"End it. She'd take away my business license."

"What?" Owen said.

"Oh, yeah, man. She's with the people, you know? Wields a lot of power. I'm like super lucky she finds me irresistible."

Geoff shimmied twice before leaning over the board and applying another layer of wax.

"Your girlfriend is Anita Moffett?"

The storeowner straightened and flipped his hair back. "You know Anita? She's something, isn't she?"

"She's something, all right."

"That girl," he said, "she took my breath away when she came in here a couple of years ago with her clipboard. She was so..."

Owen wanted to suggest several adjectives, but none of them were kind.

"Governmental," the store owner said. "I fell for her right then and there."

"And she agreed to go out with you?"

He looked at himself and waved his hands along his body. "She knows a catch when she sees one. She threw the hook in the water, and I bit. Girl reeled me in like a deep-sea fisherman."

"So you—"

"Fisherwoman."

Owen frowned.

"Fisherperson." He nodded with satisfaction.

The big man rolled his eyes.

Conspiratorially, Geoff leaned in and said, "She likes it when I'm verbally correct, you know."

"Verbally?"

"Oh yeah, man. The girl loves it when I use the right words and stuff."

"I'm sure she also loves it when you refer to her as a girl."

"Huh?"

"Did you agree to organize against Marlene Babb?"

He nervously chuckled. "Well, sure. Marlene totally harshes my mellow. She's after everyone's green, know what I'm saying? She's like a kid with candy. Always gimme gimme gimme." He mimed a child pulling candy toward himself. He stared into the distance, then mimed the candy pulling again. "Gimme gimme gimme."

"Why would—"

Geoff chuckled. "Gimme. That's a funny word, isn't it?"

"Why would you agree to organize?"

The store owner tossed the bar of wax into the air, then caught it. "Why not, yo? It seemed like a totally killer idea. Power in numbers, know what I mean? Like there's more power in more numbers, get it? I mean, more is better than less when it comes to numbers. It's science." He tapped the side of his head. "I'm not in this business just because I'm a good surfer. I've got a head for it, too."

"Obviously. So, you agreed to organize along with Headbangers and Costa Buena Chillers?"

"You met Lily yet? That lady makes the best chillers. She's like a magician with frozen ice." He leaned back and yelled, "Berry Berry Melon Blast!"

A huge smile crossed the surfer's face. Owen stared at him until the grin faded.

"Guess someone's never had the Blast because you would know what I'm talking about."

"Did you tell—"

Geoff sniffed Owen. "You smell like a melon."

Owen stared at him.

"No offense."

"Did you tell Anita about Big Al's organizing?"

"Of course, man, she's my girl. All into people power and stuff. Thought it would be right up her alley, yo."

"And what did she say?"

"She thought it was great that I was finally getting societally involved. Told me to keep it up and everything. Secretly," he glanced around even though they were the only two in the shop, "I think she likes me more for my brain than my bod, which is totally cool. When you get to this age, it's hard to keep the temple ready for visitors. Know what I'm saying?"

Owen did, and he scrunched his nose in response.

Geoff Pemberton nodded a couple of times then bent over the surfboard again. When he began chanting "Berry Berry Melon Blast" to himself, Owen decided it was time to leave.

Chapter 25

"Get him!"

Owen glanced over his shoulder to see the three skate punks from earlier, sprinting toward him. He quickly turned to face them and lifted his hands, prepared to fight. The three slowed but continued moving toward him.

They were on the boardwalk, and it was late afternoon. There were plenty of people around to witness this brazen attack.

As soon as he was near, Leader screamed and threw a roundhouse punch.

Owen covered his head with his left hand and absorbed the incoming strike on his upper arm. He stepped forward, grabbed Leader, and tossed him away. With a squeal, the punk hit the ground, then rolled for several feet.

Rail stopped in front of the big man and lifted his hands. Bruising surrounded the thin man's eyes as a result of Owen previously breaking his nose. "Now, you're gonna get it," he said, his voice nasally. He danced and flicked jabs that were too far away from the big man to pose any danger.

Hoodie, still in his loose-fitting sweatshirt, moved slowly around him, crouched as if waiting for an opportunity to tackle him. One foot moved toward the other, never crossing, then he stepped away, expanding his stance.

His shoulders swayed slightly with each movement, like a high-school wrestler.

A crowd of onlookers circled the men as they jockeyed for position. The excitement from the onlookers was palpable. Several in the group called for the men to "Fight!" but no one yelled for them to stop.

Leader scrambled to his feet and hurried back to the fray. Now, the three punks triangulated Owen.

"Terms of the deal have changed," Leader said.

"What deal?" Owen asked, slowly turning, waiting and watching the three men.

"We're not offering protection to you anymore."

"I feel safer already," Owen said.

Leader jumped at him then quickly hopped back several times. Hoodie remained crouched, and Rail continued to flick harmless jabs.

Owen was outnumbered, so he knew he wasn't getting out of this without some bumps and bruises, even from these guys. Quicker was better in any altercation, and it was always his rule to take the fight to the other guy. Don't let them have time to set a plan.

With a glance toward the two followers to keep them at bay, Owen moved aggressively toward Leader who stepped backward in surprise and bumped into an onlooker.

Keeping his eyes on his cell phone screen as he recorded the action, the citizen—an older man who wore a *Give Peace a Chance* pullover—shoved Leader back toward Owen.

"Fight!" he screamed, which caused the gathered crowd to cheer wildly.

Leader took several sputtering steps toward Owen before quickly backpedaling. When he neared the edge of the crowd, he spun and punched the *Give Peace a Chance* onlooker. This caused the older man to drop his phone.

The crowd, now fully sensing the danger associated with being too close to a fight, "Oohed" in delight and held their phones closer to the action.

Leader raised his hands in victory and shrieked at the crowd. This excited the mob further, and they cheered and clapped in response.

Hoodie and Rail moved closer to Owen before he could attack Leader again. The bigger man sensed them moving and lowered into a crouch, which caused the two to hop back. Leader joined his pals, and the three men returned to their intimidating dance routine.

"We want you off the boardwalk," Leader demanded.

"Not going to happen."

"It's happening," Leader said and turned to the crowd. "One way or another!"

The hastily assembled mob cheered with excitement.

Owen faced the onlookers, many of whom pointed their cell phones directly at him. His shoulders slumped when the realization of what was occurring hit him. Somebody would post the fight to social media, and it wouldn't be long until the Satan's Dawgs or the east coast mafia saw—

Hoodie jumped on Owen's back, which caused him to stumble toward the edge of the crowd. His face almost pressed against a young woman's phone that she held extended.

"Get him!" she shouted and shook her head with frenzied delight. Owen wasn't sure who she was cheering for, but he needed to end this fight and get away from the cameras quickly.

He reached back for Hoodie, but the smaller man wrapped his legs around Owen's waist, locking his ankles together. An arm snaked around Owen's throat.

He clasped his hands around Hoodie's arms and tried to pry them off, but the smaller man had too much leverage now.

Rail quickly stepped in from the left and punched Owen in the side of the head. The big man spun, and the cheering crowd whizzed by in his vision.

He struggled to stabilize himself as he continued to claw at Hoodie's arms, which had tightened considerably. Owen Hunter was running out of time. Very soon, the man on his back would constrict the blood to his brain, and he would pass out.

Leader stepped in now and repeatedly punched the big man in the ribs like a boxer hitting a heavy bag.

Owen spun around again, knocking Hoodie into the Leader. It didn't knock the parasite from his back, but the punk leader tumbled to the ground.

The crowd roared its approval.

The big man's world darkened, and he now only had seconds before Hoodie would choke him out. Then he would be unconscious on the boardwalk, and anything could happen. A quick thought passed through his mind—the smaller man must have had some grappling experience in his background. But there was a difference between wrestling by an established set of rules and fighting on the street.

Owen bent slightly forward, which caused Hoodie's arm to cinch tighter around his throat. With as much strength as he could muster, the big man straightened, then fell straight backward.

Before they landed, Hoodie released the tension around Owen's neck. It was as if the smaller man knew how bad the oncoming impact would be. The big man's entire weight collapsed on Hoodie, and the back of his head crunched into something soft.

Underneath him, Hoodie squealed, and his legs released their grip around the big man's waist.

As Owen rolled away, Rail and Leader kicked at him. When he regained his footing, the crowd shrieked in delight.

The big man faced Rail and sneered.

The skinny man raised his hands in surrender. "I quit," he blurted. "I don't want any more of this."

"Fine," Owen said.

"What are you doing?" Leader yelled to his cohort.

The skinny man lowered his hands and said, "I didn't mean for—"

Owen punched Rail in his already broken nose, causing the skinny punk to fall to the ground. He squeaked and kicked his legs in agony.

The crowd jeered the big man for what they determined to be a dirty move—striking a defenseless Rail.

When Owen turned to Leader, the punk said, "You think you're so lucky, don't you?"

That gave Owen pause. He'd never considered himself fortunate, especially not in his current situation.

"We're not done," the punk said, then turned and ran away, leaving his two fallen associates.

Disappointment swiftly ran through the crowd. Owen heard it in their murmurs. Several of the onlookers turned their cameras on themselves to comment about the fight they just observed.

Owen knew he shouldn't walk directly back toward his store. The smart thing would be to take the long way back. Go down the boardwalk and come in through the back of the store.

As he stepped through a ring of observers, one woman said, "You're a dirty fighter."

The big man stopped and stared at her.

She was a frail woman, a little over five feet and a hundred pounds. In her hand, her camera remained focused on him.

He should have remained silent, as there were already a dozen or more people recording the fight. Instead, Owen said, "It was three against one."

The woman lifted her phone higher to better record his face.

"That's no excuse," she said. "You're a big fella. It seemed like you were doing fine out there."

Owen shook his head and walked away.

Chapter 26

Inside his store, he sat behind the sales counter and assessed the damage to his new alias.

Three days, he thought. *It took me three lousy days to blow this cover.*

At least in Maine, it took him almost a week.

Prescott Honeywell had lived in Costa Buena for thirty years, probably had thousands of interactions with strangers, and never blew his cover.

How did I mess this up so fast?

Owen thought he was trying to be a better man. Was that the problem? Was he working against his natural inclination for violence and mayhem?

No, he thought. *I can be better than the man I used to be.*

He liked how he felt today versus the man who was the bookkeeper for the Satan's Dawgs.

The skate punks forced the recent confrontations, not him. Didn't they? Should he have backed down when the Leader first arrived demanding he pay for protection? No, he would never do that. No one should. Owen may have wanted to change many parts of his life, but standing up for himself, standing up for what was right, wasn't one of the things he wanted to excise.

What about Al Ferguson? he thought.

Owen changed the Rockafellers concept to include all classic rock, which upset the man, and they had a confrontation. He could have avoided that by not wanting more, by keeping the business stuck in the fifties and early sixties, but that would have killed him inside.

He spent enough time in prison to know only hope kept a man alive. Remove desire and a man died inside himself—in a prison of his mind. Owen wasn't willing to do that.

Besides, he didn't see changing the store's concept to be that bad, yet Big Al had assaulted him for it. To him, Owen had crossed a line, but it was a line Al Ferguson and Prescott Honeywell had drawn. Owen had never agreed to it.

But should I have honored that agreement? the big man wondered.

If so, what was stopping anyone else from coming forward and saying, "Prescott promised me this..." or "Prescott promised me that..."

Perhaps Al Ferguson would have been willing to renegotiate a new deal as Sam Peyton suggested. Maybe the two men could have reached a new, mutually beneficial agreement whereby the two records stores could peacefully co-exist again on the boardwalk.

But why would Big Al willingly give up something? It was unlikely he would have done so for a stranger he had just met, especially one who rudely demanded he could sell anything he wanted. Owen admitted he hadn't acted much in a spirit of cooperation when he first met Big Al, but he didn't know the pact between Headbangers and Rockafellers existed until it was too late.

No, he finally decided, *I did the right thing by standing up for myself.*

The right thing did not feel like vindication, though. Especially since it meant Detective Cochran considered him a suspect in Big Al's murder, which he then made worse by breaking into the man's store.

Now, he'd just brawled in front of a crowd armed with cell phones. Owen dropped his chin to his chest. His secret was about to get out into the digital universe, and there was nothing he could do about it.

That wasn't true. There was something he could do about it.

He picked up the store's telephone and dialed a number.

It was answered after the first ring. "Ace Adventures, where your journey begins. How may I help you?"

The woman's voice was cheerful.

Why are they always so pleasant when I call in?

Anyone calling this number was doing so because of bad news.

"I'd like to speak with Mr. Onderdonk," he said.

From the other end of the line came clicking on a keyboard. "Mr. Onderdonk is away from the office currently. Would you like to leave a message?"

"He visited my rental earlier today."

More keyboard clicking.

The door to the store opened, and a cool breeze wafted in.

Sam the Scavenger stood in the entryway. He wore a multi-colored Baja jacket but still had on his board shorts and dirty running shoes. Noticing the big man was on the phone, Sam waved and headed toward the cat who lay in the middle of the store.

"I see he was out there," the woman said. "Did he forget something?"

"Let him know I caught a cold."

"A cold?" the woman said.

"I think it's about to go viral."

More clicking.

"I'll get him the message," the woman on the phone said, "but you probably should take some cold medicine, though."

"Okay."

"Maybe lie down. That always helps when I'm not feeling well."

"Thank you," Owen said.

"Or you know what I like—"

He hung up without waiting for further health recommendations.

Sam scratched Travis behind the ear. As he did, the tom lifted its head into his hand. "You sick, Hunter?"

"No."

The rotund man straightened and put his hands on his hips. "You told that person you had a cold and that it's about to go viral. I don't want to catch nothing."

"You listening to my phone calls, Sam?"

"No."

Owen stared at the store's visitor.

"I guess, yeah."

"I'm not sick. I'm trying to cancel a reservation, is all."

Sam nodded. "I hear ya. Been there myself once or twice. Over-promising and under-delivering, am I right?"

Owen tilted his head.

The visitor waved away the comment. "Doesn't matter. I heard what happened on the boardwalk. You okay?"

"I'm fine." He slipped off his stool and walked around the counter. "There were three of them. They jumped me."

Sam's eyes widened as he stared at the big man. "Did you kill them?"

"What?"

"Is that *blood*?"

Owen glanced down at his red-stained T-shirt and jeans. "No."

"Looks like blood," Sam said, leaning in with concern in his eyes. He sniffed twice. "You smell like a melon."

"I had an accident at Costa Buena Chillers. Some kid with a big, red drink—"

Sam tilted his head back and hollered, "Berry Berry Melon Blast!"

The cat scampered away.

When the visitor's gaze returned to the bigger man, his smile faded. "You don't enjoy the frozen concoctions?"

Owen shook his head.

"You're missing out, my friend. They're life changing."

"Obviously. I've got a question for you, Sam."

Seriousness descended on the smaller man's face. "Not again."

"Where did you get the albums you sold me? And don't tell me you got them from a thrift store in Rancho Camaro."

"Chimera."

Owen's face flattened.

Sam pointed at the big man's shirt. "You *swear* that's not blood?"

The big man folded his arms over his chest. "I got arrested, Sam. There's a detective who likes me for Big Al's murder."

"You didn't do it, right?"

"I didn't, but I got multiple milk crates of albums in here with the same price tags Al used in his store."

A nervous smile crossed Sam's lips. "That's an eerie coincidence, isn't it?"

"No, it's not."

"It's not?"

"*Sam.*"

The smaller man sighed. "It's not what you think."

"You killed Al."

"No!" Sam said. His hand slipped under his Baja jacket to rub his belly. "Al was my friend. I wouldn't do that to him."

"So, how did you get into the store?"

"He gave me a key."

"Why would Al give you a key?"

"We were friends for a lot of years. Whenever I fell on hard times, he'd let me sleep in the attic."

Owen remembered the cot and tightly rolled sleeping bag. He'd thought it had been for Al to sleep there, but perhaps it was for Sam instead.

"How often have you fallen on hard times?"

"Whenever I can't find a place to crash."

"So, where do you normally sleep?"

"Wherever the wind takes me."

The big man leaned forward. "What's that mean?"

"Sometimes I sleep on the beach. Sometimes a couch. Sometimes a lovely lady will take pity on this old—"

Owen held up his hand. "Enough."

"I'm still a man."

He smirked. "When you were in Al's attic, did you see the map on his wall?"

"The map of the boardwalk? Sure. What about it?"

"Did Al tell you what he was doing?"

"He was organizing the boardwalk businesses to go after Marlene."

"You didn't think of telling me this earlier?"

"Well..."

"Sam!"

The smaller man's eyes widened.

"Why didn't you tell me about this?"

"Al swore me to secrecy," he said. "I wasn't to tell no one what was going on."

"And did you? Remain silent, I mean."

"Of course. It was Al. He was good to me. I wouldn't do nothing to hurt him."

"Except steal from him after he was dead."

Sam pursed his lips. "I didn't mean to lie to you, Hunter."

"You didn't mean to lie?"

The smaller man chuckled. "I guess I did mean to, yeah. But it wasn't malicious."

"You remained silent so you could hide the fact that you stole from a dead man you claim to be your friend."

Sam's face slackened. "When you put it like that..."

"I am."

The smaller man looked down at his dirty shoes. "Doesn't sound so good."

"No, it doesn't."

Sam put his hands into the front pocket of his Baja jacket. "You needed some albums, and it wasn't like Al was going to need them anymore. No disrespect intended. I figured I could earn a few bucks since it wouldn't be long before I couldn't stay in the attic. Somebody was bound to change the locks."

"Why didn't you steal money from the till? You could have cut out the middleman—me."

Sam frowned. "I guess I never thought of that."

Owen shook his head. "If Detective Cochran finds these albums and realizes they're from Headbangers, I'm done for. Do you realize that?"

The smaller man glanced at the milk crates. "That wouldn't look good, would it?"

"Unless I tell him about you, that is."

The visitor's face whitened.

"You should probably go. I've got some thinking to do."

"Listen," the smaller man said, holding his hands up in protest, "you don't have to do that. I'll take them back. I'll put them where they belong."

"If the cops catch you going into Al's store, two wrongs aren't going to help either of us."

Sam lowered his eyes. "I guess you're right." He turned toward the door but stopped. "Hey, can I say goodbye to Yerchoise?"

"Another time."

He nodded and strolled quietly to the door. "I'm sorry, Hunter. I didn't mean to cause you any problems. You're a good guy."

When Sam the Scavenger left, Owen walked behind the counter and started the computer. When the FBI Rats website popped up, he hurriedly went to his page and scrolled down to check his whereabouts.

He still worried the mob might be able to track him through the computer, but he figured if that were the case, maybe it was like a phone call. That he had to be on for a certain amount of time before they could triangulate his position. He only needed to be on the website for a moment to see if his status had changed.

At the bottom of his page, his whereabouts were still listed as *UNKNOWN*.

Quickly, he closed the Internet browser and stared at the blank screen. The cold sweat had returned to the base of his neck.

Chapter 27

Grill, You Know It's True was once again nearly full. Owen stood patiently behind a couple near the door. Every seat in the establishment was taken. He could have eaten elsewhere, could have eaten some quick-serve ramen at home for that matter, but he wanted to talk with the Grill brothers about their involvement in Al Ferguson's plans for a boardwalk union.

Most of the patrons inside the small diner didn't linger over their dinners. They hurriedly ate with their heads down. Whenever they looked up, it was to smile with a mouthful or nod appreciatively to their dining partner as they chewed.

Horace, the hunched-over server, walked past the tables, quickly cleaning up after anyone who finished eating. From one table, he grabbed the plates from a young thirty-ish couple who remained seated, holding hands across the table, cooing affection to each other.

"Go," he said, motioning his head toward the door.

"We just finished," the man said, clearly irritated. "We'd like a moment to sit and talk."

"Talk elsewhere. Some customers want this table."

The man looked Horace up and down. "We don't want to leave. Not yet. We have a right—"

"Gerald!" the server yelled.

The diner suddenly fell silent as everyone stopped eating. The assembled patrons turned to stare at the interaction between Horace and the insolent customer.

The short-order cook, his white apron dirty with grease and other foodstuff, scrambled from behind the grill. He gripped a metal spatula in his fist.

The irritated customer's wife leaned across the table. "Let's go."

"No," he said. As his face reddened, his eyes remained on Horace. "We don't have to."

The wife leaned in with a pleading look. "But I don't want to get—"

When Gerald arrived at his brother's shoulder, Horace jerked his head toward the impertinent customer and announced, "Banned!"

"Banned?" the man whined.

"Banned," the wife complained.

"Banned!" Gerald said with an emphatic pump of the spatula in the air.

"Now, get out," Horace said. "Make room for new customers."

"But this was where I proposed to her during college," the husband said as he absently reached for his wife's hand. Not looking at her, he didn't realize she had pulled her hands back and now angrily glared at him. "This is our place for special occasions."

"Too late!" the short-order cook called out as he hurried back to the grill.

"The rules," Horace said. "Know the rules."

The wife stood and glowered at her husband. "What did you do?"

"Too late!" Gerald yelled again from behind the grill.

"The rules," the server said.

The husband silently trailed his wife as they shuffled past the other customers, who now eyed them with mouthfuls of food and shaking heads.

Horace waved at the two well-dressed men in front of Owen and pointed to the table. The two hurried in, sat, and immediately ordered.

A woman at the bar finished her meal, said her thanks to the server, and left. "Your turn," she said to Owen.

As he slid onto the stool, he said to Horace, "You guys are tough."

The server crossed his arms. "Don't like? Eat someplace else. We don't have the time."

"It's okay."

"Of course, it's okay," Horace said. "Look at how many people are here. If it wasn't okay, they wouldn't come. Eat by the rules or go elsewhere."

"Speaking of rules."

"You talking or eating?"

"Can't I do both?"

"Order first."

"You guys got a special?"

"What do we look like?" Horace turned to Gerald and yelled. "The special," he yelled and walked off to fill a glass of water. When he returned to Owen, he clunked the glass in front of him.

"Now, you can talk."

"You joined with Al Ferguson on unionizing against Marlene Babb."

Horace stuck his tongue between his lip and teeth, wiggling it back and forth.

"No comment?"

"Was that a question? I figured you're telling me things I already know."

"Why didn't you tell me about that when we first met?"

"I did. I told you Al talked about organizing against Marlene and ended up dead. I suggested you keep your thoughts to yourself."

"You didn't tell me you and your brother agreed to be part of Big Al's organization."

Horace shook his head. "That was none of your business. A lot of things are none of your business. Do you want to know what I ate for breakfast? Probably not. How about my cat? Would you like to know about my cat?"

"Why would I want to know that? I don't even like *my* cat."

The server frowned. "A man who doesn't like his cat is like a man who doesn't like his mother. He isn't worth knowing."

Owen remained silent.

Horace smirked. "Too close to home?"

"Your business, Costa Buena Chillers..." Owen ticked off on his fingers. He paused, waiting for Horace to lean his head back and chant an affinity for the frozen concoction. Instead, the server slowly blinked as he waited for him to continue. "And Seaside Surf Gear joined with Big Al to go against Marlene."

Horace glanced around, unimpressed by what Owen was telling him.

"Why hadn't the other businesses joined?"

The older man's gaze returned to him. "Because he had just started. He hadn't had time to talk with the others."

"I saw the attic of his store where the map was."

The server's eyes slanted. "How did you get in there?"

"It was unlocked."

"I doubt that."

"Why was Rockafellers exed out?" Owen had his own beliefs in the matter, but he wanted someone else to share theirs.

The older man inhaled deeply before answering. "Because Prescott was dead."

"Oh. I hadn't thought of that. The recruitment started after he died?"

"Didn't matter none. He didn't want to be involved, anyway."

Owen leaned forward on his elbows. "Because he owned his building?"

"Sure."

"What is it, Horace?"

"Prescott, God rest his soul," Horace crossed himself and kissed his thumb, "he didn't think he needed to participate. It could happen to any man. Not me or Gerald, because we are smart in here." He tapped his temple. "But Prescott, he got soft-headed. Too much time in the sun and sand."

"Okay."

"He ended up like the one who owns the surf shop."

Owen thought about the stoned-out philosopher Geoff Pemberton waxing his surfboard.

Horace turned his attention to two men sitting idly at a table as they read their cell phones. "You two are finished," he called. "Make way for new customers!"

The two frantically stood. "Sorry, Horry!" the first one called.

"Yeah, sorry," his friend said. "See you next week."

They hurried out of the restaurant.

"Horry?"

"You don't get to call me that."

"Why not?"

"I'm not sure about you."

"How's that?"

"You're here, asking questions about Al and Prescott, both who are gone and can't defend themselves."

"I'm trying to find out what happened to them."

"Why? Why do you care so much? Are you a policeman?"

"No."

"You supposedly run a record store, but I see you walking around the boardwalk. I see you fighting with the hoodlums. When do you have time to run a store? When do you have time to make any money? You must be rich like Prescott. He never ran the store either. Instead, he swam and surfed all the time.

There must be a lot of money in selling old records."

"I'm not rich."

"Then you should be inside your store. Let the police do their work. You do yours. Everyone will be happy."

"What if someone gets away with murder?"

"It's America," Horace said. "Everyone gets away with murder."

Gerald walked out from behind the grill and set a plate on the counter. "The special," he said, before walking back into the kitchen. On the plate was a length of toasted French bread. In the middle of the sandwich was a mixture of hamburger meat and cheese. Owen thought he smelled onions inside.

Owen picked up a knife and fork. "What is it?"

"A French bread sandwich."

Owen cut a piece of the concoction and shoved it into his mouth. "This is good."

"Of course, it's good. That's why it's the special."

While Owen ate, Horace continued.

"The problem with Prescott was he played too much. Surf, swim, walk on the boardwalk. He never worked in his store for lots of years. When Big Al came to him about standing up to Marlene, Prescott said he didn't want to be involved. He had no reason to do so. She didn't own his building, so there was nothing for him to do. Al thought otherwise, but let it go. We were all very disappointed because we liked him, but Prescott always did his own thing."

Owen would have the same problem while in the WitSec program. Was he forever destined to be an outsider wherever he went?

"Then Prescott drowned, and you showed up. Your first impression of Al didn't go very well, and then he died. Now, nobody is organizing against Marlene."

"Maybe we should start," Owen suggested.

Horace gave him an appraising look. Finally, he said, "Maybe you should shut up and eat your special before you get banned."

Owen nodded, dropped his eyes to his plate, and cut another piece of the sandwich.

Chapter 28

"You're Marlene Babb's nephew."

Titus Forsberg leaned back in his chair. "What about it?"

"Why were you in my store?"

"I like old music."

A line of album covers ringed the upper wall of the bar. Owen noticed the two albums that the hipster had purchased earlier.

At eye level were a variety of photos. Some were in color, but most were monochrome. He stood to examine them.

In every photo was the same man. In the black and white pictures, the man was young and had hair. In the color photos, he was bald and jowly. Throughout them all, though, his eyes were intense.

Owen tapped his finger near a photo. "Bartholomew Babb?"

"My uncle."

Celebrities populated the photos. On each frame was a small strip of brass indicating the personality with Bart. The names were legendary—Frank Sinatra, Dean Martin, Ronald Reagan, Henry Kissinger, and Eddie Van Halen.

Eddie Van Halen ate here, Owen thought.

He touched the photograph and smiled. He turned to Titus, who studied him with intense interest. His grin faded, and he returned to his chair.

"So Bart bought up the properties along the boardwalk?"

"Over time, yes."

"He must have been a very wealthy man."

"On paper."

"Never had cash lying around?"

Titus shook his head. "He poured every dime back into buying the other properties. Never spent a nickel outside his business or the properties."

"Nickels and dimes. Why would he do that?"

The hipster considered his answer before speaking. "Aunt Marlene pushed him. That's not uncommon knowledge, so I'm not speaking out of turn."

"Why would a man let himself be pushed that way?"

"Marlene was an attractive woman, almost twenty years younger than Bart. He wanted to keep her happy, and happiness for her was buying up the properties on the boardwalk." He pointed over his right shoulder. "There's a picture of them with Johnny Weissmuller, the original Tarzan. He visited Bart's Place once. Check it out."

Owen stood again and stared at the color photograph. He understood who Bart was now and guessed the man standing with them had once played the Lord of the Jungle, but it was the young Marlene who gave him pause. She looked like Marilyn Monroe in a black sweater and white pants. Red lipstick popped from the photograph. Her beauty commanded attention.

"She was something back then, wasn't she?"

"Yeah," Owen muttered.

"That's why Uncle Bart worked so hard. She was young and beautiful, and he wanted to keep her happy. But she didn't want trips or fancy jewels. She wanted security. She wanted the boardwalk."

"And he hustled for it?"

"Every day until he died. And he lived until he was eighty-three. When they met, he already had a couple of properties on the boardwalk and a couple of businesses. Together, they built a Costa Buena empire."

"Did they have kids?"

"No kids."

"Then why build it?"

"Because they could."

Owen frowned. "Where do you come into this?"

"Marlene needed someone to manage this."

"You said you manage situations."

"I'm handling this along with the Babble."

"Among other things, right?"

He smiled. "She's slowing down and asked me to start learning the portfolio."

"I'm assuming you knew about the organizing that Big Al was doing."

"That was a recent development, but I wasn't too worried about it. What could they do? Each tenant has a lease. They either follow the contract, or they could get out. It's simple. If they don't like something, they can take it up with their attorney or a priest."

"Did she ask you to kill Prescott, or did you do that on your own?"

Titus Forsberg laughed. "Prescott drowned. How could we be involved with that?"

"I don't know yet, but you wanted his building."

"That doesn't mean we killed the man. Besides, he had agreed to sell it to Marlene."

"Nothing was signed, though."

"They had a verbal agreement and were working to finalize an actual sale document. I don't understand your accusation, Mr. Hunter, but the fact is our attorney drafted the paperwork. No, Prescott hadn't signed it, but he stated he would. Then he died. His death was an inconvenience to us. The only one who looks suspicious in this matter is you. You showed up a couple of weeks after his death. There's no way that property could have cleared probate in time for you to claim ownership. Yet here you are."

Owen had no idea what probate meant, but he kept his face flat as if he were bluffing in a game of poker. "So, who killed Prescott?"

"Who said anyone killed him? He had a surfing accident and drowned. Even the police said so."

"I'm not so sure."

"Are you the police?" Titus asked. "I thought you were a record store owner."

"I am."

"Well, Mr. Record Store Owner, sometimes an accident is really an accident."

"Maybe. Maybe not."

Titus shook his head. "Even if we wanted to, and I'm not saying we did, how would we stage a surfing accident?"

"I don't know," Owen said as he stood. "But when I figure it out, I'll be back."

Chapter 29

Back home, Owen sat at the kitchen table and began another letter to Daphne Winterbourne.

After the day's events, especially the fight with the punks and the crowd of filming onlookers, he fully expected his secret to be exposed soon. If that were the case, two things were possible. Either he would move to a new location as a precaution, or the Satan's Dawgs would find him. He didn't like either idea.

In his letter, he shared what he'd been up to. He wasn't supposed to do this, of course. It was against the rules of the Witness Protection Program, but he wanted to remain connected to Daphne.

He hoped she still cared. He even wrote that in the letter.

When he finished, he sealed the envelope, stamped it, and put it to the side. He then reclined on the couch to replay the events of the past three days.

What did he know?

Prescott Honeywell drowned in a surfing accident. There was a bump on his head that the police believed was caused by his surfboard. Water was inside his lungs. The police had ruled it an accidental death. Maybe it was what it seemed. Only the fact that Owen showed up as the new owner of Rockafellers made it look suspicious. Perhaps he should accept what the police thought about his death and move on.

On the other hand, there was no questioning that Big Al Ferguson had been murdered inside Headbangers. Someone had clubbed him over the head with an Elvis Presley statue. Whoever killed him, and why they wanted him dead, was still a mystery. It could have been because of his threat to organize the local businesses against Marlene Babb, or it could have been a completely random killing.

Involving himself in the hunt for a killer was a silly preoccupation. He wasn't a trained investigator. He didn't have the skills for such a task. It was quite the opposite. Detectives are trained to think about problems carefully. As a bookkeeper, Owen had been trained to act quickly and decisively, letting the chips fall where they may. Working this mystery without the tools he normally had at his disposal made him feel clumsy.

When he was a Dawg, he kept a list of transgressors against the club. Then he removed those folks from the list. Sometimes it was clean. At other times, it was messy. But it didn't require a lot of forethought. If someone crossed the club, they paid dearly for it. There wasn't much investigation required.

That's why he struggled to figure out this problem. It wasn't natural for him. It was hard and made his head hurt. Besides, everyone he was dealing with was a citizen, except maybe for the punks. They were more of an irritant than anything else. Using actual violence against any person he contacted so far was out of the question.

His thoughts drifted back to Marlene Babb. She was Al's landlord, and she wanted to buy Prescott's building. Both men were connected to her, although Prescott's relationship seemed thinner.

Of course, all the other businesses on the boardwalk had the same link to Marlene that Big Al had. This included Costa Buena Chillers—*Berry, Berry, Melon Blast!*—Seaside Surf Gear, and Grill, You Know It's True.

This tenuous connection didn't mean that Marlene was any more the killer than Titus Forsberg, the hipster nephew. Although, that weird little guy did strike Owen as someone who could be involved in something nefarious.

All the possible connections didn't change the predicament in which he currently found himself.

Albert Ferguson was murdered, and Owen was still a possible suspect for it.

This morning, Detective Cochran said he was going to investigate Owen's past. He wondered what tomorrow would bring. He hoped the detective would have been too busy today to do much about it, but he doubted it. The detective seemed likely to stay after Owen until he had all the answers he wanted. He would be like a dog with a bone.

The Dawgs, Owen thought.

If any one of them saw the video of his fight with the punks, they would be on the way.

If so, would they alert the FBI Rats website, and would a broadcast go out, bringing killers from the east coast mafia?

In that case, would it even matter who killed Albert Ferguson?

Yes, he decided, it would still matter.

Because Owen Hunter was not a killer.

Beauregard Smith killed many who deserved it after crossing the club, but Albert Ferguson wasn't the type of man who needed a visit from a bookkeeper.

Owen didn't want that death associated with his name.

He remained on the couch but eventually closed his eyes and went to sleep.

Chapter 30

The morning didn't bring Owen a refreshed perspective.

Instead, he awoke with a sense of foreboding—the same feeling he had before he was sent to prison. It was also the same feeling he had before he agreed to turn rat for the FBI.

He showered and dressed, hoping a new perspective would come with a soaping and a shave. It didn't.

Breakfast didn't help either. He ate alone at a little diner off the boardwalk. No one spoke to him, and he didn't look to anyone for conversation. While pushing his eggs and hash browns around the plate, he thought about knitting again.

The act of knitting brought him peace during stressful times like this, but he hadn't been able to venture out and buy a new kit. He briefly had a bag in Pleasant Valley but had to dispose of it along with a body. Purchasing a skein of yarn and a pair of knitting needles wasn't necessarily a priority while fleeing killers on a motorcycle.

And when he arrived in Costa Buena, knitting didn't seem to be necessary. He thought he was going to be in a friendly, calm environment. He'd been wrong. There would be no time to buy a kit today. He had other, more pressing priorities.

The boardwalk was quiet as if it were the morning after a long party where everyone felt the aftereffects of too much alcohol and excitement. Las Vegas mornings felt this way, and Owen wondered if the Costa Buena boardwalk experienced this every day. He'd have to get out here early again to know.

Along the pier, the Ferris wheel remained quiet, and only a few die-hard fishermen stood along the rail with their lines cast into the water.

Several surfers rode the Pacific Ocean waves.

The sun was low in the east, which created shadows along the building storefronts.

As Owen walked, he moved into the sun's rays and felt the warmth on the right side of his face. He closed his eyes and allowed himself to smile. The simple act of being in sunshine brought him a renewed sense of hope. Maybe things would work out okay.

When he opened his eyes, an older woman in a light blue jogging suit speed-walked toward him. Her arms pumped back and forth, and her hips swayed to the side as she hurried along. She wore a purple baseball hat that compressed her silver-hair down over her ears.

Owen nodded and cheerfully said, "Good morning," even though he didn't necessarily feel the morning was good, nor did he feel cheerful.

The speed walker's face pinched. "Creep." She hurried by and angrily glanced back after she passed.

His smile faded, but he pressed on. When he reached his record store, he stopped in surprise. In front of his store, three women marched in a circle with picket signs clutched in each of their hands.

He slowed when he heard their chant. "Heck, no! Make him go!"

As he approached the small group, he saw Anita Moffett loudly leading the cheer. The two women behind her, both in their early seventies, wheezed slightly each time they chanted and sucked deeply for air when they finished. They pumped their signs up and down as they walked.

Their handmade signs each carried a different message.

Costa Buena Doesn't Fight!

And *Costa Buena Loves.*

And his personal favorite, *Costa Buena - Leave it Be!*

When Anita saw him, she loudly said, "He's here, ladies."

The two older women flanked her as they blocked the entrance to his store. The three rested their signs on their shoulders much the way a baseball player would rest a bat.

Owen eyed the three women, then their picket signs. "What's this about?"

"It's about you, Mr. Owen. Of course."

"About you," the first older woman said.

"Of course," the other added encouragingly.

Anita nodded. "That's right."

"What about me?" Owen asked. "What did I do?"

"You can't be that dense," Anita said.

The two women tittered. "Dense," they said together like schoolgirls sharing a secret.

"I have no idea what you're talking about."

"Fighting, Mr. Owen. You were fighting."

"Fighting," the women agreed. One of the ladies mocked several little jabs in front of her.

"I have the right to protect myself."

"Not according to the pamphlet I gave you." Anita rolled her eyes, then glanced at her support team. "Which you clearly did not read."

"I read it," Owen said. He thought about the tri-fold pamphlet that he tossed in the garbage with barely a glance.

Anita's attention snapped back to him. "You read it?"

"I most certainly did."

"If you read it, then your fighting is an even more egregious violation than we thought."

"More egregious," the first woman agreed.

"Than we thought," the second added.

"What are you talking about?"

"Not reading and not knowing the rules is one thing, but reading the pamphlet, then casually flaunting a total disregard for those rules, shows a complete lack of respect for our community."

"Total disregard," one woman said.

"Lack of respect," her friend whispered.

"Okay," the big man said, holding up his hands in surrender. "Maybe I didn't pay as much attention as I should have."

"You didn't pay attention to the rules of our community?" Anita asked. "You don't think enough of Costa Buena to follow our most basic rules?"

"Basic," the women said, shaking their heads.

Owen's face warmed. "I have a right to defend myself," he said half-heartedly.

"Call the police," Anita said. "That's what they do—protect and serve. As a business owner, you do the same, but different—serve and protect. Serve the customers and protect the community. You didn't do either, Mr. Owen. And because of that, we are protesting both you and your business."

"Did Marlene put you up to this?"

"Marlene?" the older women asked, concern in their voices.

Anita turned to them. "He thinks Marlene is behind the murder of Mr. Ferguson."

The two women gasped, then covered their mouths.

"And the drowning of Mr. Honeywell."

"Monster!" the first woman said.

"Vile," her friend stammered, "Vile. Despicable."

"She's controlling you," Owen said. "All of you."

"Mr. Owen—" Anita said, but she was cut off by the hissing of the two older women. They mimed scratching him as if they were cats with claws.

"Ladies," Anita said. "Show some restraint."

They yanked their hands back but continued to bare their teeth.

"Marlene Babb had nothing to do with this protest," Anita said. "It was, and is, totally motivated by *your* actions. We are responding to the things you've done, the things that were posted online last evening, and the hateful social media comments made about our beautiful community. We must protect Costa Buena at all costs."

"Protect it at all costs?"

"That's right," Anita said. "We've already filed the request that your business license is pulled. Now, we're here to protest your store until the city closes you down. We're going to let the citizens know just exactly who you are."

The two women hissed at him.

"I need to open my store," he said.

"Go right ahead," Anita said. "We'll be here all day."

The women parted, allowing him access to Rockafellers.

Chapter 31

Travis reclined near the window and watched with curiosity as the picketers marched outside the store. The group of three had grown to a circle of twenty. Each woman furiously waved a handmade sign with every step.

It was only 10:00 a.m.

A television news crew—a female reporter and a male camera operator—stood nearby and interviewed Anita Moffett. They positioned the camera to get Rockafellers in the background.

When Owen first walked into the shop that morning, he went directly to the windows to pull the shades. Unfortunately, he was quickly reminded that one set had fallen, and the other was missing its middle.

Therefore, he stood behind the counter and did his best to remain out of sight of the picketers.

"Giving them an audience only emboldens them," Owen said.

The tom ignored him, though. Travis clearly found the ladies more interesting than what was occurring inside the shop, which, at that moment, was nothing.

So far, no one had dared to cross the picket line. There had not been one customer in the first hour of business.

That might have been normal on any other day of the week, but twenty angry women protesting outside his business put a considerable damper on Owen's attitude.

He logged into the FBI Rats website to check on his status. He scrolled to the bottom of his page. His location status still showed *UNKNOWN*.

After shutting down the Internet browser, he turned on some hard rock music. If there were no customers today, he'd at least enjoy the solitude by cranking the stereo.

Crunchy guitars squealed from the speakers hanging about the store. Travis jumped, his head turning as he searched for the source of the irritating noise. Deciding the music presented no immediate danger, the tom turned his attention back to the parade of picketers.

Owen was antsy and left the privacy of the counter to pace back and forth inside the shop. He occasionally stopped to view the scene outside, hoping the crowd would soon dissipate. Seeing they hadn't, he would grunt and continue his circular path.

The camera crew signaled additional trouble. Their presence alone meant he couldn't leave through the front, but he wanted to work on the murder of Al Ferguson.

Being stuck inside Rockafellers this morning felt like a prison sentence.

That was an exaggeration, Owen admitted to himself. Being in the business alone was far better than prison. Maybe the better analogy would be house arrest. He had once worn an ankle bracelet that tracked his every movement, so this concept was the same.

He couldn't leave the store without exposing himself to the news camera. He could slink out the back, but that felt wrong, like he'd done something inappropriate. And he'd already been exposed to several cell phone cameras during the fight with the punks.

How much worse would getting seen by television cameras make it?

Owen stopped pacing to shake his head at that thought.

There was dumb, and then there was stupid.

Fighting in front of a crowd was dumb. Walking outside the store with a news crew waiting for him was just plain stupid.

A large man in blue jeans and a western shirt walked through the picket line. He held the hand of a woman who trotted behind him, her eyes scanning the crowd. The crowd of picketers jeered and angrily pumped their picket signs at the two people who dared cross their line.

Federal Agent Max Ekleberry held the door open for the woman.

She wore a black jean jacket, a beige knit shirt, black jeans, and beige boots. Her short hair was tucked behind her ears. Hoop earrings dangled almost to her shoulders.

Several women on the picket line turned toward the store, yelling in anger.

When Ekleberry stepped in, he said, "I see-" but stopped suddenly to look toward the speakers pumping out loud heavy metal music.

The woman with him rolled her eyes.

"Good Lord!" Ekleberry yelled as the door swung closed. "That's loud!"

Owen reached over the counter to turn the music off.

The federal agent and the woman moved into the middle of the store.

"You made some friends," Ekleberry said, jerking his head toward the window. The protesters had stopped screaming at the store and had returned to marching in a circle.

"I fought with some local punks, and the community do-gooders think I should be a kinder, gentler business."

"We saw the fight," the agent said. "It's all over social media."

"How bad?" Owen asked.

"Bad," Ekleberry and the woman said in unison.

The agent tilted his head toward his guest. "Owen Hunter, this is Cherry Lane."

The big man smiled and stepped toward the woman. They shook hands.

"Cherry Lane?" The big man asked. "Named after?"

"The Van Halen song?" The woman shook her head ruefully. "Yeah. My dad was a complete dork for their music."

Owen was impressed. "That is so cool."

"Not really. Since we were already the Lanes, it didn't take much imagination to name me this. My dad said he wished I would have been a redhead. I don't think he understood how genetics worked, though."

"Still. Must have been cool to have a father like that."

"You would think, but he listened to his music like you—loud and annoying."

"That's how you're supposed to listen to it."

"When you're fifteen," she said, squinting at him. "Not when you're in your forties."

Owen's smile faded. "I'm nowhere near forty."

Ekleberry chuckled. "I promised Cherry a trip to Costa Buena to do some shopping, but she had to give me a few minutes to catch up with an old friend."

"Is that my cue to leave you two?" she asked.

"I'll only be a few minutes, baby," the agent cooed. Owen fought back his disgust. "Then I'll come join you. I promise."

The woman leaned in and kissed the lawman on the cheek. "Find me when you're done," she said.

Ekleberry watched her leave. A wistful smile formed on his lips, and his eyes grew soft. Cherry waved at him before exiting, and he wriggled his fingers at her.

Disgusting, Owen thought. When the door closed, the big man said, "She seems nice."

The G-man turned to Owen, and his gaze hardened. "What were you thinking?"

"What do you mean? I said she was nice."

"Not about her, ding dong. About fighting on the boardwalk. You realize you're all over the internet?"

"It's that bad?"

"The video—no, *videos*—popped up on several sites I follow. It's viral, Beau. The Costa Buena Beat Down they're calling it. Three against one. It's gotten a lot of attention. Made the national news."

"The national?"

Ekleberry nodded.

"I was only protecting myself."

"You need to be smarter."

"From a public ambush? What would you have done differently?"

"I don't know, but I'll tell you this—you're on the clock."

"With the Dawgs, you mean?"

"If I saw it, then they saw it. The mob, too."

"I figured."

"Onderdonk called me. He's setting up an emergency move for you. He's in full panic mode."

Owen walked around the store. "But I'm not ready to leave."

"What are you talking about? When Ted's ready, you're moving."

"But I haven't figured out Al Ferguson's murder yet."

"What about it?"

"The police suspect me."

"So?"

"I didn't do it."

"I know, but the beautiful thing is—you're not you."

He stared at the FBI man. "Excuse me?"

"When the marshals move you, Owen Hunter disappears." Ekleberry snapped his fingers. "Just like that. You'll get a new life. You'll be someone else." He clapped his hands, turned his wrists over repeatedly, then waved them in front of him, like a dealer at a blackjack table. "No worries."

"But I'll know. And that will always bother me." He tapped his chest. "In here."

Ekleberry frowned. "Who are you?"

"What do you mean?"

"This wouldn't have bothered the bookkeeper."

His face relaxed. "I'm trying to be a better man, Max. Haven't you ever wanted to be better? To change who you were?"

The lawman's eyes drifted toward the door. Owen wondered if he was thinking about Cherry Lane. If so, what did he want to change for her?

"I didn't kill Ferguson," Owen said, "and I don't want people thinking I did. I'll own what I've done in the past, but I don't want to be labeled a murderer for someone I didn't kill."

Ekleberry nodded. "Know this then. Owen Hunter is on borrowed time. When Onderdonk shows up, Hunter goes. Understand? The U.S. government has a lot invested in you, Beau. We don't want you playing footsie with the hippie crowd and end up dead in return."

"I hear you. When Onderdonk arrives, I'll go.
Now, did you get the information I asked for?"

Chapter 32

When lunch was brought in for the protesters, Owen realized the demonstration wouldn't end before the afternoon.

A group of silver-haired ladies, all of them wearing purple hats and colorful outfits, showed up. The newcomers smiled and laughed as they passed out handmade sandwiches wrapped in wax paper.

Several of the late arrivals hugged the protesters as if they were friends that hadn't seen each other in quite some time. The protest had turned into a Costa Buena social gathering.

Now, more than forty mostly silver-haired women gathered in front of Rockafellers. Some marched. Some chatted. And throughout the festivities, all would occasionally glance with disdain toward the music store.

The gathering also attracted a second news crew. They set up their camera to film the front of the store. Many of the protesters took turns being interviewed by the reporters.

Nearby, a juggling mime tossed several oranges into the air while a clown tied balloon animals together for children.

Owen now stood just inside the store's front window, watching it all. He was no longer afraid of the protesters seeing him or even the cameras making him out. His face had been on social media and had been splashed on the national news. Ekleberry already told him he was on borrowed time.

What more could happen?

Travis lounged nearby in the window, and Owen absently scratched behind the cat's ear.

Many of the silver-haired women ate while they marched. This quieted the chanting for a time. For that, Owen was grateful. He had turned off the store's music during Ekleberry's visit, and it had remained silent since.

Passersby on the boardwalk stopped to film or photograph the demonstration, often ensuring they got the shop in the background.

A woman wearing a purple hat stepped into the picket line and took the place of a protester, who then hurried toward Rockafellers.

The protestor, slightly hunched over from age, opened the door and smiled kindly at Owen.

"Mind if I use the loo?" she said, slightly out of breath. "I'll never make the pier."

He wanted to tell her no, that she could squat in the ocean for all he cared, but she reminded him of his grandmother.

"In the back," he muttered. He jerked his head in the general direction.

She stepped into the store and scuttled off.

As the demonstrators quietly marched, many pumping their half-eaten sandwiches up and down, Owen's mind drifted to what Ekleberry had just told him.

Marlene Babb nee Winkler was not the innocent, civic-minded woman he'd initially thought her to be. She had an extensive criminal history before marriage. It was petty crime mostly—thefts and shoplifting—but she was once charged with extortion—a felony—which never resulted in a conviction.

After her marriage to Bart Babb, however, Marlene never again committed a crime.

Had she turned a corner? Owen wondered.

Or had her crimes become more sophisticated when she moved into the white-collared world of real estate? Those acts of corruption were something Owen didn't know about.

The misdeeds in which the Satan's Dawgs were involved were never that sophisticated. He wished he understood how the fat cats of Wall Street got away with defrauding the public, only to be protected by the government when the economy crashed. Those were the real crooks.

Perhaps Marlene had figured out that game.

And Samuel Peyton's story was what he figured it would be. His criminal history was littered with low-level crime—malicious mischief, burglary, theft, shoplifting, public intoxication. There'd never been a break in his string of arrests. He was seventy-three years old and had a criminal history fifty-seven years long. None of it ever violent, though.

He couldn't imagine Sam being involved in either Prescott Honeywell's death or Al Ferguson's murder.

"Is that your kitty?"

Owen's eyes slid to the silver-haired woman, who stood very close to him now. He hadn't heard her return from the restroom. Her eyes were bright as they focused intently on Travis. The big man pulled his hand back from the cat, surprised he'd been petting the mangy thing.

He thought about ignoring the woman, but she indeed reminded him of his grandmother, so he chose to be kind. "You can have him if you want."

"Oh, no, dear. Every boutique needs a kitty." She reached out and gently touched his ear. "What's his name?"

"You get to pick."

The woman's smile faded. "Excuse me?"

"You see," Owen said, gesturing toward the tom, "a cat is a reflection of whoever they're with at the moment. Therefore, that person should be able to name it. The only caveat is the name has to be a musician."

"But we're both here."

"I've already picked my name. Now, you can pick one. For *you*."

Her smile remained soft as she lightly touched the cat. "We can't have two names for the kitty, or he'll be bipolar, or manic-depressive or something that little tom-toms aren't meant to be."

"It's a cat," Owen said with a shrug. "He's not going to care. It's not like he's a dog."

The woman reeled back in horror. "That's not—" She turned to the cat. "He's a—" She pointed a slightly crooked finger at him. "Why you— I'm telling the others!"

She scooted toward the door, yanked it open, and was gone.

Through the window, Owen watched the older woman scurry outside, waving her hands as she went. The protest suddenly stopped, and the mass of women gathered about her. The other women in purple hats pulled in tight—substantial concern registered on each of their faces.

The hunched-over woman wildly gestured as she spoke, pointing back to the record store. When she finished speaking, all the women turned and faced Rockafellers. Grimaces and anger flashed across their faces.

Anita Moffett studied the store for a moment before walking away.

"I don't think they like me," Owen said as he absently scratched behind the cat's ear.

Travis wagged his tail.

Chapter 33

"I know what you are."

Detective Roy Cochran stood in the middle of the record store. With his hands hooked into his belt, his sport coat was pushed back to reveal not only his badge and gun but also his sagging belly.

"Yeah?" Owen asked. "What's that?"

"A killer," he said flatly. "A stone-cold killer. Maybe the worst to set foot in Costa Buena."

"You've got me confused with—"

"You're also a rat."

Owen stayed silent, but his heart raced, and he could hear the blood pumping in his ears.

"You were an enforcer for an outlaw motorcycle club based in Phoenix, Arizona."

"I'm not sure where you're getting this story, but—"

"The California Bureau of Investigation, that's where. They picked you out pretty darn quick when I told them about your tattoos."

Owen's eyes flicked to his hands and arms.

"A tattoo is as good as a fingerprint with you types," the detective said. "As a member of the law enforcement community, let me be the first to say we appreciate you giving us a bunch of additional ways to identify you."

Outside, the protest continued. Along with the Welcoming Committee and the women in purple hats, a new group had joined the demonstration—Costa Buena Paws for Peace.

Younger women holding signs with cute cat pictures paraded among the picketers.

The protest chant had changed, though. Now, the group was hollering, "Bad for Buena! Bad for Cats! Get Out!" over and over. They weren't even trying to be clever.

Another camera crew had joined the event, making three news networks covering the protest.

Several costumed characters roamed the crowd, taking selfies with the protesters. There was a Spider-man, a Darth Vader, and a woman dressed as a Disney princess.

Children dashed through the crowd with overly large frozen concoctions in one hand and a string tied to a helium-filled balloon in the other. Frazzled parents ran behind them.

Owen's window for solving Big Al's murder and getting out of Costa Buena was quickly vanishing. Especially with a homicide detective now standing inside his store.

"If you've found out that information," Owen said, "you must know why I'm here."

"Witness protection, right?"

"I'm cooperating with the Feds."

Cochran rested his hand on his gun. "That doesn't mean you're not still a killer. Once you get it in your nostrils—"

"I'm trying to be a better man," Owen interrupted.

"A better man? You broke into Al Ferguson's business. That sounds *better* to you?"

"I was trying to find out who killed him."

"Look in the mirror."

"I didn't kill him."

"I don't believe you."

"I'm telling the truth."

"The truth? You're a rat, Beau Smith. That means you'll lie."

Hearing his real name come from the detective was disconcerting. "I'm not lying about this. Talk to Agent Ekleberry."

"I will. Believe it. If he tells me anything I don't like, I'm arresting you for the murder of Al Ferguson."

"On what proof?"

Cochran rubbed his face and studied the big man.

"So wait. You're not arresting me now?"

"If I do it now, your federal buddies will just come and pull you out. No, when I arrest you, it'll be for good. You can make book on that."

"I didn't do it."

"You keep saying that. Then tell me who did."

"I'm working on it."

Cochran sucked something imaginary through his teeth before saying, "My money's on you."

"Detective, if I wanted to run, I would have. I could have the moment you showed up asking questions. Or after Agent Ekleberry got me free. I could have done it this morning when they showed up." Owen pointed outside.

The detective glanced through the window to the protest.

"But I've stayed here trying to figure out who killed Al Ferguson. I'm even working on who might have had a hand in Prescott Honeywell's death."

"That was an accident."

"Maybe it was. Maybe it wasn't. Who knows?"

"I do. So does the coroner."

Owen waved his hands. "The point is, I could have run at any time. I could have ditched this cover, and no one would have been the wiser."

"I would have been."

"Now. Sure. But the government wants me to leave Costa Buena, and I've fought them to stay. Why would I do that if I killed Big Al?"

Cochran rubbed his face again. "Why *would* you do that?"

"Because I don't want to be accused of being a killer."

"You *are* a killer."

"But I didn't kill *him*. Detective, I've taken responsibility for the men I've killed in the past. That's how I ended up here. Ask Ekleberry."

Detective Roy Cochran crossed his arms. "Okay, tough guy, if what you're saying is true, tell me what you know so far."

Chapter 34

It was late afternoon, and he hadn't eaten anything since breakfast.

He didn't want to leave the store to get something. The camera crews were a deterrent, as were the angry women picketing him.

To make matters worse, a group of about fifteen skateboarders joined the protest now. They pumped their skateboards up and down while the entire mob marched in an ever-widening circle. Hoodie and Rail were with them. The two punks smiled and waved toward Owen whenever they passed in front of his store.

He left the window and found a list of local eateries near the computer. He placed a couple of calls, hoping to get something delivered to the store. Unfortunately, as soon as he gave his address, the employees told him there was no way they were crossing the picket line.

"Bad for business," one employee said and abruptly hung up.

"A dog is not a cat!" another employee yelled, and the call ended.

After that, he figured he would skip eating until later. He'd only missed one meal, so it wasn't like he was going to die of starvation.

He tapped the computer's keyboard and called the screen to life. After starting the Internet browser, he checked the FBI Rats website. His location still showed *UNKNOWN*.

He closed the browser and moved back to the windows.

With the demonstration occurring outside—Hoodie and Rail waved again—and the three camera crews recording it, he wondered how long the *UNKNOWN* status would remain. It wouldn't be long now until someone realized it was him in those videos. He needed to get moving before this changed.

The cat strolled into the middle of the store and sat. The big man stared at him. Travis seemed fat and content as he set to cleaning himself.

"Who feeds you?" Owen asked.

The tom's hind leg stuck straight out as it ran its tongue across it. The big man scrunched his nose.

A light, almost tentative knock at the back door caused both Owen and the cat to turn their attention to the rear of the store. The cat stood and took several curious steps in that direction.

"Wait here," he said. "I'll see who it is."

The cat turned in circles as Owen passed by.

In the hallway, he heard another knock, this one more forceful than the previous. There was no peephole to check who was back there.

Perhaps it could be a news reporter wanting to get an interview.

Or perhaps it was one of the Dawgs, hoping to get the drop on him.

Maybe it was the leader of the skate punks. He still hadn't shown up to the protest. Perhaps he had snuck around to the alley.

Owen wasn't worried about another confrontation unless, of course, the guy brought a weapon.

Or could it be Onderdonk wanting to avoid the protest out front? He surely wouldn't want to pass through an angry mob of purple-hatted women, cat-lovers, and skateboarders.

All these possibilities passed through Owen's mind within a second.

Lastly, he thought about yelling, "Who's there?" but that just felt weak.

He grasped the knob and slid open the lock. The big man yanked open the door but remained prepared to slam it shut if necessary.

Standing there, looking slightly sheepish, was Anita Moffett. She held a sandwich wrapped in wax paper in her left hand and a plastic bag of homemade chocolate chip cookies in her right.

"Mr. Owen," she said.

He stared at her.

"I'm sorry," she said. The words seemed hard for her to say.

"For?"

"For how this has blown completely out of proportion."

"I figured this is what you wanted."

"I wanted you to be a better businessman." She held up the sandwich and cookies but didn't hand them to him. Instead, she walked by, down the hallway. "I didn't want to run you out of town."

He shut the back door, secured it, and followed her into his store. She stood near the counter, out of the line of sight of the protest. It was then she offered him the sandwich and cookies. He wanted to say no, but his stomach gurgled.

He took the food and mumbled, "Thank you."

"You should thank the ladies from The Purple Hat Coalition. They brought the snacks."

"Purple Hat Coalition?"

"They're a militant group of elderly ladies. Sixty years and over."

"Militants?"

"They look for causes to support by bringing homemade goodies."

Owen removed one of the cookies from the plastic baggie and bit into it. "They brought sandwiches and cookies," he said around the mouthful. "How bad can they be?"

"Don't you see?" Anita said, pointing toward the window. "That's how Costa Buena protests have such amazing stamina. Whenever one starts to tire out, the PHC arrives in the nick of time. If it starts to rain, they'll bring ponchos. If the sun comes out, they'll bring sunscreen and umbrellas. The PHC has chapters around the nation. They're fanatics for this stuff."

Owen studied the woman. "I thought this type of thing would be right up your alley."

"Quite the opposite, Mr. Owen. My goal is civil obedience. I want people to play by the rules and help each other out. I want everyone to get along for the common good."

"And the purple hats? What do they want?"

"*Sustained* civil disobedience."

Owen stared at the remaining cookie. He didn't want to eat it considering The Purple Hat Coalition's goal of sustained civil disobedience. However, if those ladies were going to keep up their strength, he better as well. He glanced out the window and took another bite of the cookie.

"Why are you telling me this?" he asked.

"Because I want results. My ladies want results."

"But isn't Marlene part of your crew?"

"We didn't want her to join us. I tried to tell you that, but you didn't believe me. We're a volunteer organization, and she forced her way in."

"Then why did you tell her about Al Ferguson organizing the boardwalk?"

Her face blanched. "I did no such thing."

"You're seeing Geoff Pemberton."

She blinked several times before saying, "I didn't know that was public knowledge."

"He told me when I visited his shop."

She shook her head. "He talks too much."

"What do you see in him?"

Anita shrugged. "He has a kind soul."

"And that kind soul told you about Al's plans to organize against Marlene, and then you told her because she's the benefactor of your committee."

Her face hardened. "I didn't tell anyone anything, especially not her. As I said, I want everyone to be civilly obedient. Had I told

Marlene, something like this would have happened. I wouldn't want that."

Owen studied her. She seemed sincere. He turned to the crowd outside.

"Can't you call this off?"

Anita shoved her hands into the pockets of her slacks and watched the crowd. "The protest is no longer about us wanting you to behave in a manner according to the Welcoming and Standards Rules and Regulations."

"What is it?"

She walked over to the cat and bent down. "You're a good boy, aren't you, Cat Stevens?" She glanced back at Owen, then turned to pet the tom again. "Out there, everyone has a different agenda, Mr. Owen. It's anarchy. Paws for Peace is upset about what you said. Did you suggest a cat is less than a dog?"

He watched Anita pet the tom. In an earlier interaction, she had been deeply upset by the naming rule, but now she seemed hardly bothered by his assertion that Travis wasn't as good as a dog.

"Did you really suggest such a thing?" she asked again.

"It was a joke."

"So you brought their hatred on yourself," Anita said and stood. She moved near the counter. "And the skateboarders? Supposedly, they're protesting your treatment of their friends."

"They tried to extort me. *And* threatened me. *Then* they attacked me."

"They're telling a different story to the news crews. If you want to stand up for yourself, you should go out and tell your story."

"I can't."

"Why not?"

As he thought, he watched Travis bat around the little Elvis head. He must have found it again. "No matter what I say, it won't matter. No one will hear me above the yelling. The best thing I can do is remain quiet."

"That's what The Purple Hat Coalition thrives on," Anita said. "Silence. They'll continue to bring sandwiches. Then they'll bring blankets for tonight. They'll keep the pressure on you."

"What did I do to them?"

"To the PHC? Nothing. But it's sustained civil disobedience they're after. The cause is irrelevant."

"I'll withstand them."

"No, you won't."

Owen turned back to the window and watched the crowd of angry women.

"Why not slip out the back?"

"And slink away?" he asked. "I won't do that."

Anita Moffett inhaled deeply as a sadness crossed her face. "You're a strange one, Mr. Owen. I'm sorry that this has spiraled out of control."

He studied her. He didn't understand her sudden change in demeanor. He wanted to tell her that she was a strange one as well, but instead, all he said was, "Thank you."

After she left, he shut the back door and
relocked it.

Chapter 35

The door to Rockafellers opened, which allowed the aroma of the ocean and the noise of the protest to drift in. Marlene Babb stood confidently in the doorway. Sitting cockeyed on her head was a large-brimmed purple hat with a red feather stuck in its band. She wore a dark blue pantsuit and black flats.

"Mr. Hunter," she called out. "Hasn't this been the most glorious of days?"

From behind the counter, Owen said, "You and I have very different definitions of glorious."

Marlene walked inside and stopped in front of the windows. With her hands on her hips, she watched the marching crowd outside. Picket signs, large photos of cats, and skateboards bounced up and down in the air as the mob circled in front of his store.

Owen ambled over to stand near her. The cat wandered out then and sat to watch them.

"Just glorious," she muttered.

"What do you want, Marlene?"

"I'm here to talk about our demands."

"Demands?"

"I'm the official representative for the protest."

"You? Did you volunteer?"

"Of course," she said. Her smile was broad and toothy.

"What do they want?"

"Where to start? The Welcoming and Standards Committee wants you to abide by their Rules and Regulations."

Owen folded his arms over his chest. "I have no plans to do that."

Reveling in the moment, she nodded once and winked. "Atta boy," she said.

He frowned. He didn't like Marlene encouraging his behavior.

With a glance toward the tom, she said, "And Paws for Peace wants you to release your cat to them. They want to find him a loving, responsible pet parent."

"Pet parent?"

"Their words. Not mine."

The cat ignored them both and set to cleaning himself.

Owen's lip curled, and he shook his head. He never wanted the darn thing, but there was no way a bunch of feline zealots could bully him. By pushing him into a corner, he was forced to utter bitter-tasting words.

"He's my cat," Owen said. "And I'm not giving him up."

Marlene's smile faded as she watched the cat. "Not sure why you'd want such a mangy thing, but—" Her smile returned now. "Fight the good fight, Mr. Hunter."

Holding back a sneer, the big man asked, "And the skateboarders?"

"I'm not sure why they're out there, except they said they want to support us. Kind of a sweet gesture, actually."

"And The Purple Hats?"

"Oh, honey, we're already getting what we want," she chuckled.

"Sustained civil disobedience."

Marlene smiled broadly but kept her attention outside. "You've heard about us."

Owen said, "This is all a smokescreen. None of it matters."

"How can you say that?"

"Because you've moved these pieces into place, except for maybe the skateboarders. You've moved everyone into place to force my hand to get me to sell out."

She turned to him. "You give me too much credit. I don't control the Welcoming and Standards Committee."

"You're a part of them."

"Hardly. Oh, I've wanted to influence what they do on the boardwalk, of course, but I don't make the rules. I can't get Anita to do anything I suggest. She's too darn headstrong. Often flying off the handle and doing her own thing. She's going to get herself into trouble one day. And how would I know you would be so foolish as to insult a cat? Don't you know the tabby is the official animal of Costa Buena?"

"You're kidding me."

"Look it up. This city adores its cats."

"I didn't know that."

"The pride of our boardwalk, our Ferris wheel, is El Gato Grande—The Big Cat. What further evidence do you need?"

"I'm not selling this building," he said.

Her smile returned. "I was hoping you would say that."

"Why?"

"Because of this," she said, gesturing toward the activity on the boardwalk. "This will keep everyone else in line."

He watched her, so Marlene continued.

"The other businesses, Mr. Hunter. They were organizing against me." She glanced over her shoulder. "You know about it, of course."

"But how do you?"

"I know everything that happens down here. Even though I didn't have a hand in planning this, the whole debacle should show the others not to mess with me. Sometimes the illusion of power is just as good as real power."

They remained quiet for a time as they both watched the mob outside.

"Why do you want this property so badly?"

"Because I want them all."

"What does it matter? You can't redevelop the boardwalk. Costa Buena has laws governing against that."

She shrugged. "Did you play *Monopoly* when you were a kid?"

"Sure."

"Remember the rules? You play until you get all the properties, or you bankrupt your opponents."

"Who are you going to leave it all to? You don't have children."

"Why does that matter? Sometimes, we play the game only to play the game."

"What motivates you when you already have so much?"

She smirked. "Because it's there, Mr. Hunter. Haven't you ever done something simply because you wanted to do it? Why do people climb Mount Everest? Why do others jump out of airplanes?"

He hadn't done either, so he shrugged.

"Because they can. Because of the challenge."

"What happens to the properties when you die?"

"Are you planning on killing me, Mr. Hunter? I didn't take you for the overly violent type."

Owen smiled. It was the first time she had misjudged him.

"If you must know, the portfolio will go to my nephews, Titus and Paul."

"Nephews?" He had only heard mention of one nephew.

Marlene's attention stayed focused outside on the protesters. "My little sister came late to our family. I was almost twenty by the time she was born, so she and I hardly knew each other. We were sisters in title only. She grew up and had a couple of boys. One was a smart kid. Great head on his shoulders. The other was a bit touched if you know what I mean." She glanced at the big man. "A lot like his mother, truth be told."

Her focus returned to the marchers. "She passed a couple of years ago, leaving those boys with no family but me. So I invited them out. The oldest came first. He's a bit of an oddity. He's almost thirty now, so one can only hope he grows out of it sooner rather than later. I'd like him to learn the family business."

"Is that why you put him in charge of Bart's Place?"

"You mean Titus. No, he's the one with a head for business. He came after Paul was already out here for a bit. Titus has a lot of potential. He'll go far. The properties and the businesses will be in good hands with him."

"He told me he was hired to manage situations."

"That's true. Along with managing the properties, he's trying to integrate his brother into polite society."

"Integrate how?"

Marlene chuckled. "Paul is an acquired taste. He's into skateboarding and that awful punk rock music. He's got a number of those silly piercings. The boy looks like a darn pincushion if you ask me."

Owen scanned the assembled mob to find that the punk leader had rejoined his two friends.

"There he is now," Marlene said and waved to her nephew.

Leader waved back. Hoodie and Rail waved along with him.

"Those boys look like a bunch of misfits," Marlene said, "but deep down, they're good kids."

Owen watched them. "They're grown men."

"Kids to me," she said. "Titus has taken his brother under his wing, helping him learn how things are supposed to work around here. Someday, both of those boys will take over if Paul can ever move beyond this silly phase of his."

Outside, the three punks slipped out of the mob and wandered off down the boardwalk.

The woman stepped to the door and placed her hand on the knob. "Just so we're clear— you're not going to sell the building, is that correct?"

"That's correct," Owen said. "I'm not selling."

"Atta, boy," Marlene said with a smile. "Keep up the good fight." Then she yanked open the door and yelled, "More sandwiches, ladies! He's not cooperating."

The mob yelled in delight.

Chapter 36

Owen watched him cross the picket line. He waddled as he struggled to carry two boxes of albums. He grasped the lowest one tight to him and balanced the upper box against his chest. The horde of women jeered and hollered as he passed through them.

Samuel Peyton winced with each rude comment tossed his way. Near the front of the store, he glanced angrily over his shoulder and shouted something. Several of the women in purple hats raised their fists and yelled back.

Owen met him at the door, opening it as he arrived. Sam hurried in, whispering a strained, "Thank you" before setting the boxes in the middle of the floor.

"Those women!" he said and pointed to the window just as a sandwich was thrown against the window. It exploded apart and left a residue of mayonnaise and mustard. A slice of American cheese remained stuck to the glass.

"What did you say to them?"

He rubbed his forearms. "I only said that their purple hats make them look like eggplants. But that's because they called me a scab for crossing their picket line."

Another sandwich slapped into the window, followed immediately by a third one. A Rorschach test of mayonnaise and mustard now covered one window. Two slices of cold cuts hung on the glass, along with the slice of yellow cheese.

Two silver-haired women, their faces scrunched in anger, screamed profanities at the window.

"Seems they didn't take that comment very well."

Sam stuck his hands into the front pocket of his Baja jacket and watched the women hollering at him. "Can you imagine what it's like to be married to a woman like that?"

"Haven't given it much thought."

"I'll tell you," Sam said, leaning back as another sandwich splatted against the window. "It's gotta be great! All that fury. Wow! Really something."

Owen's brow furrowed.

"I've been married three times, and none of them had that type of energy." Sam's eyes brightened as he watched the gathered women angrily holler toward Rockafellers. "Got me a mind to go out there and meet number four."

A seagull descended and attacked the yellow cheese on the window. Within seconds, a flock of the birds descended to attack the cold cuts and sandwiches that now lay in front of the building. Several of the women ran toward the birds, wildly swinging their picket signs.

The cat ran to the window and yowled in delight at the activity.

Sam acknowledged the tom with, "Hiya, Yerchoise," but he kept his eyes on the women battling with the seagulls. "Think those sandwiches were any good?"

"They were."

The visitor's eyes drifted to the big man's. "If they're eating good and they have a common enemy, this protest isn't likely to die down soon."

Owen leaned against the counter. "Not likely."

"I brought you some more records."

"Not stolen, I hope."

Sam frowned. "No, not stolen. I really got these from that thrift store in Rancho Chimera."

The cat leaped from the window to attack the small Elvis head that lay near the base of a display rack.

Owen knelt and flipped through the albums in one of the boxes. None of them were marked with price tags. All the records were out-of-order alphabetically. He nodded with satisfaction and straightened.

Sam leaned over to see what the cat was batting about. "Disrespectful," he mumbled.

"Marlene was just in here," Owen said.

The visitor turned his attention to the big man. "What did she want?"

"To threaten me."

"Into selling the store?"

"Uh-huh."

"She was never right once she got around money."

"You said you knew her before she married Bart Babb."

He nodded. "She was my girl way back when."

"Your girl?"

"That woman broke my heart."

"How was that?"

"She was destined to be the first Mrs. Samuel Peyton. I proposed to her and everything, but then she met Bart and dumped me. After her, I was never the same."

"Why didn't you tell me?"

"Because it's embarrassing."

"What's so embarrassing?"

"Look at my life compared to hers."

"What about it?"

Sam shrugged. "She dumped me when she got her hooks into ol' Bart. She rode that poor man to his death and ended up the richest woman in Costa Buena. But me, I refused to do things her way and got kicked to the proverbial curb. I got married three times, one right after the other, and each of those ladies followed Marlene's example."

"Kicked to the curb?"

"I was there so often I could have been a fire hydrant."

Owen smiled politely.

"After the last divorce, I've spent my life wandering up and down the boardwalk, living on other people's scraps." Sam picked up the small Elvis head and wrapped his fist around it. "Marlene's well-respected, and I'm... a scavenger."

"I'm sorry for calling you that."

"It's all right," he said. "It's what I do, right?"

"She said she knew about Big Al's gathering of the businesses. Who could have told her?"

"Not me. I would never do that to Al, and I sure as heck wouldn't tell her. We don't talk. She pretends I don't exist."

"So the only others who knew about the meeting were the owners of Costa Buena Chillers, Seaside Surf Gear and Grill, You Know It's True."

"And the killer," Sam said. "Al was killed in his store, right? Maybe whoever did it had time to go into the attic and see the map of the boardwalk. They could have figured out what was going on. Isn't that possible?"

"Right," Owen said.

"But you don't think Marlene had anything to do with his death, do you?"

Owen pointed to the protesters. Several of them continued to swat away seagulls. "She's responsible for that mob, Sam. Why couldn't she be responsible for a man's death?"

Sam's face scrunched.

"What?"

"I thought you were responsible for that out there."

Owen's eyes narrowed.

Sam nervously chuckled. "I get what you're saying, though. Marlene is out there rousing the rabble, so to speak. I hate the woman as much as I hate athlete's foot, but I don't see her killing Big Al. She's more of a manipulator, if you see what I'm saying."

"Do you think she could have convinced someone else to kill Al?"

Sam shrugged. "Maybe. It depends on the man, I guess."

Owen immediately thought of her nephews, Titus and Paul. He would need to get some further information about them.

Sam rolled the little statue head back and forth between his fingers. "This is shameful, man. Doing this to The King. I know you hate the oldies but have some respect for the greats." The smaller man's shoulders slumped before he set the little Elvis head on the counter. "I'm gonna head out the back. I don't need to make the eggplants any angrier than they already are."

"I thought you liked them that way."

Sam's smile was full of regret. "After talking about Marlene and my divorces, if I want to get married again, I should have my head examined."

Chapter 37

Shortly after five, another wave of The Purple Hat Coalition arrived. These silver-haired women came prepared for an extended battle.

At the front of the procession, two women carried a long folding table. With a flourish, they set it on its side, extended its legs, then flipped it upright in front of his store.

Behind them, another woman carried a clear plastic tub. She opened the box, and the three women set the table. A white cloth was removed, flapped open and draped over the table. Then a stack of paper plates, cups, and plastic flatware were neatly arranged.

The three women stepped back as the next group of purple-hatted women arrived. They carried a variety of crock pots, tins, and Tupperware containers and spread them over the table before removing the various lids.

One of the ladies removed a long multi-outlet extension cord from the plastic tub. After plugging the crock pots into it, she glanced around for an outlet. Meeting Owen's gaze through the window, she smiled and politely waved.

"Excuse me," she said, peeking her head inside the door.

He stared at her.

The elderly woman lifted the extension cord and smiled. "Mind if we borrow a little power?"

"You're protesting my store and me."

"But our crocks won't stay warm."

Owen shrugged. "How's that my problem?"

Her face darkened before she turned to the assembled crowd. "He won't let us have power!" she hollered.

The protesters jeered, and another half-eaten sandwich slammed into the window. A brave seagull dove toward the food, but several of the picketers angrily swatted at the bird.

"Now, look what you've done," the woman said and closed the door.

For Owen, that was the signal to close the store for the day.

He locked the front door.

****

He slipped out of the back and into the alley.

He hated to do it as it felt like he was slinking away, and honest men didn't do that. He'd done plenty of skulking in his previous life as a Satan's Dawg, but he wanted to conduct his business out in the open now. No more underhandedness.

However, he wasn't going to walk through that mob and pass by the assembled news crews.

That left him with only one choice.

On the opposite side of the alley were small bungalow homes. The unpaved driveway was dusty and rocky. Weeds cropped up along the rear of the commercial buildings and the fences of the houses.

At the end of the alley, behind the last building which he knew to be Bart's Place, Titus and Paul—the hipster and the punk—stood outside.

Owen dropped to his knee and tucked himself as tight as he could next to a building.

He couldn't hear what was being said between the two men, but he watched the interaction.

Titus pointed an angry finger at his brother, who only shrugged in return. The hipster wildly gestured as he spoke. This went on for several moments.

In the end, Titus shook his head, yanked open the back door to Bart's Place, and went inside.

Paul, the leader of the punks, stared at the closed door for a moment, then shook his head and left the alley.

Owen waited there for several moments, considering what to do next.

Chapter 38

The next morning, Owen woke early. It wasn't difficult, as he'd hardly slept. Concern about the Dawgs arriving in the middle of the night continued to plague him.

He'd packed his clothes and personal effects and stored them in the trunk of the white Toyota Tercel. It was dented and rusted, and he'd only driven it when he arrived in town. It burned oil and was a gutless wonder. However, it wouldn't stand out in a crowd.

Owen headed toward the boardwalk and stopped by a mailbox on the way. He dropped off another letter to Daphne. In it, he let her know that he was going to have to go on the run, so he might not be able to stay in touch for some time.

He felt the warmth of the morning sun on his face as he approached his store. The protest was still going on. The crowd was slightly smaller, but there were plenty of picket signs and cat pictures bouncing up and down as they marched in a circle. A group of women in purple hats handed out coffee and donuts.

He sighed and walked toward a nearby business, shimmying along the side of the building before slipping into the alley. He hurried along the back of the boardwalk until he came to his store.

When he stepped into Rockafellers, he heard voices and immediately froze. In turn, the voices stopped talking.

Travis appeared in the hallway, his tail slowly moving to and fro. Owen didn't know who was inside his store, and he wasn't about to risk a meeting with a member of the Satan's Dawgs. He waved his hand at the cat and tried to encourage him to come down the hallway.

Instead, the tom dropped to the ground. Its tail flopped lazily up and down.

Owen smirked. *This is why dogs are better.*

A head poked around from the corner. "Beau?" U.S. Marshal Ted Onderdonk studied him. "What're you doing back there?"

A second later, FBI Special Agent Max Ekleberry appeared over the marshal's shoulder. "Yeah. What're you doing?"

The two men watched Owen walk slowly toward them. Concern was deeply etched on both of their faces.

"Where've you been?" Onderdonk asked.

"Taking a walk," the big man said.

"This is no time for personal reflection," the marshal said. "The Dawgs are on the way."

Owen didn't worry. He knew this was coming. He walked behind the counter and tapped the computer. As the machine whirred to life, he asked, "How far out are they?"

"Couple hours, maybe. They got a good head start at about midnight. We had local PD watching them."

He called up the Internet browser, entered the web address he knew by heart and watched as the FBI Rats website popped up.

Onderdonk said, "You know what it's going to say."

Owen scrolled until he found his name. His status was updated to *COSTA BUENA, CA.* It repeatedly flashed red.

"You're all over social media," Ekleberry said. He turned to look out the window. "How did you cross the purple hats?"

"Playing hard to get."

Onderdonk tilted his head. "Come again?"

"The woman who wants to buy this building. She's one of them, and I told her no."

"Those ladies are members of The Purple Hat Coalition," Ekleberry asked.

"So?" Owen said, closing the web browser. "You're not going to tell me they're a domestic terrorist group, are you?"

"Not that," Ekleberry said. "But we do watch them. They're all about sustained civil disobedience."

"I heard that, but what exactly does that mean?"

"Think of it as your grandmother's version of anarchy."

"Takes all types," Owen said. He grabbed the little statue head that sat on the counter. He absently played with it as the men continued to talk.

"With the Dawgs on the way, your cover is blown."

"There's also a local detective who figured out who I am."

"Roy Cochran?" Ekleberry asked.

Owen stared at the little head he held between his fingers. He slowly turned it left and right, then he held it to the light.

The marshal clucked his tongue against the roof of his mouth several times. "I'm going to get in trouble for this."

"Maybe not," Owen muttered, carefully placing the Elvis head back onto the counter.

"How's that?" the lawman looked from Owen to Ekleberry.

"If we solve a murder before you pull me out, that's got to look good to your supervisor."

"How do we do that?"

"I'm close, really close, to figuring this whole thing out."

"Beau..." the marshal said.

"A couple of hours. That's all I'm asking. Then we'll go."

"That's cutting it too close."

"Please," Owen said. "I don't want to slink away and let people accuse me of the murder of Al Ferguson."

Ekleberry and Onderdonk traded glances. Both shrugged in response.

"Thank you," the big man said.

"Don't thank us yet," the marshal said. "How do you plan to prove this?"

"Max," Owen said, turning to the FBI agent, "can you get Detective Cochran down here? I'd like him to be a part of this."

"I still have his phone number. I can give him a call." The lawman pulled his cell phone from his pocket and walked away to place a call.

"Ted, here's what I need from you."

Chapter 39

It was the most crowded the store had been since he'd taken over Rockafellers. Of course, he'd been here less than a week, so there wasn't much history to judge by.

Detective Roy Cochran wandered about the store. His eyes darted around as if he was searching for something. He stopped by the front counter and picked up the little head of the dancing Elvis. He held it up to lights and studied it intently. When he put it down, he stepped off to the side and made eye contact with Owen. Cochran nodded twice.

Anita Moffett and Marlene Babb huddled together. Owen had called and requested their attendance. Anita wore a dark blue pantsuit, while Marlene wore a long dress and another purple hat. This one was extremely extravagant, though, as if she knew she was about to be the center of an event.

Samuel Peyton stood by himself. He'd dressed for the occasion. Owen had called and told him to dress for guests. He wore a Baja jacket, a white turtleneck, dirty jeans, and ratty tennis shoes. It was his version of California business wear.

Several business owners were in attendance. Geoff Pemberton of Seaside Surf Gear chatted with Lily Brummett from Costa Buena Chillers. Brothers Horace and Gerald Grill stood together and grumbled about closing the restaurant for this meeting.

Standing by himself was Titus Forsberg from Bart's Place. He remained stoic and watched all the activity with wary eyes.

Marshal Ted Onderdonk and FBI Agent Max Ekleberry stood near Owen. Both G-men wore their guns and badges today.

"Ready to go?" Onderdonk asked. He held a white envelope near his leg.

"Almost."

The marshal frowned, then tucked the envelope into his back pocket.

"We don't have time for a party," Ekleberry said, tapping his watch. "The Dawgs are less than an hour out. You've got to wrap this up and fast."

Marlene noticed the three men talking. "Got something special planned for us, Mr. Hunter?"

He lifted his hand and smiled.

The door to the store opened, which allowed the heavy aroma of the Pacific Ocean to sweep in along with the continuous chanting of the protesters.

Officer Santiago arrived with Paul Forsberg, the leader of the skate punks. Outside the store, Hoodie and Rail stood with their faces pressed against the windows.

When Santiago released Paul, the skater reluctantly headed toward Titus. The hipster rolled his eyes and shook his head. The Forsberg brothers stood together, but neither acknowledged the other.

"Now, we can begin," Owen said. "Thank you for joining us this morning."

"Like we had a choice," Paul muttered.

"Why are we here?" Marlene demanded.

"We're here," Owen said, "to find Big Al's killer."

Most mumbled some type of denial, and Owen lifted his hands for silence.

"Detective Cochran," the big man said, "can you tell us all how Big Al was murdered?"

The detective studied Owen for a moment, suspicion clearly on his face. Finally, he said, "Blunt force trauma."

"How about something a little less technical? They may not know how Al really died."

Cochran turned to those assembled and said, "He was hit over the head with an Elvis Presley statue."

"Killed by The King," Agent Ekleberry said.

"A *fat* Elvis Presley statue," Owen clarified.

"So disrespectful," Marshal Onderdonk whispered.

Sam leaned toward the marshal. "That's what I said."

Owen stepped into the middle of the room. "Many of us had some reason to dislike Big Al."

Again, most murmured a denial.

Owen lifted his hands for silence. "Big Al was organizing a protest against Marlene and her, shall we say, tough business practices."

Marlene nodded approval for his choice of words.

Owen continued. "Al gathered these folks," he waved toward the assembled business owners, "in his crusade, which angered Marlene when she found out."

The business owners glanced at one another, then averted their eyes. Marlene half-shrugged at the accusation.

"By the way, Marlene, how did you find out?"

She shrugged. "Al told me himself. It was better to let everyone think that I had a spy. Breeding a little distrust among the masses keeps everyone in line."

The business owners glanced at each other.

Onderdonk tapped his watch, then made a couple of circles in the air with his finger.

"Anita Moffett," Owen said, hurrying things along, "complained that Big Al continually refused to follow the community rules and flaunted his disrespect for such."

When everyone turned her way, she straightened and focused, as if pulled from her thoughts. "He was a miserable man," she said quietly. "And he wasn't good for the community."

The cat wandered out and joined Owen then. Most everyone smiled at the tom.

"Paul was squeezing Big Al for protection money."

"Paul!" Marlene said. "Why would you?"

The bald punk shrugged. "Relax, Aunt Marlene. I didn't kill the man."

Owen said, "And he didn't come up with the idea of protection money on his own. He was doing it at the direction of Titus."

"Titus!" Marlene said. Her face reddened. "How could you?"

The hipster shrugged. "We were only earning a little extra."

"But protection money? These people had leases." She glanced away for a second, then turned back. "That would only aggravate a hornet's nest!"

"They had help from Paul's friends," Owen pointed to Hoodie and Rail, who still had their faces pressed against the window next to the dried mayonnaise and mustard smears. Both men's eyes widened when everyone inside turned to look at them. "Who among you paid the protection money?"

Lily, Geoff, and the Grill brothers all raised their hands.

"I was scared," Lily said.

"They said they'd burn down my store if I didn't pay," Geoff said.

The Grill brothers shrugged and said in unison, "The cost of business."

Both Paul and Titus dropped their heads. Outside, Hoodie and Rail ran away.

"Was Big Al paying?" Owen asked the Forsberg brothers.

"He refused," Paul muttered. He quickly added, "But we didn't kill him."

"We swear," Titus added.

"I believe you," Owen said.

"You do?" the Forsberg brothers said in unison.

Detective Cochran stepped forward. "You do?"

Owen winked at the detective. "Trust me."

"But you extorted these businesses," Cochran said to the brothers. "For that, you're under arrest." He yanked out a set of handcuffs and handed them to Officer Santiago. "Hook these two up and take them out to your car."

As Officer Santiago placed both men in handcuffs, Marlene Babb stepped forward. "I demand—"

"No," the detective said, "you don't get to do that today. Let Santiago do his work. You can see these two down at the station."

Marlene reluctantly stepped back. Along with the other assembled guests, she watched her nephews get searched.

The door opened, and a female officer entered. She scanned the occupants of the room before proceeding directly toward Detective Cochran. After the uniformed officer handed the detective a brown paper bag, he whispered something to her. She moved near the front door where she stood to survey the proceedings. Cochran held the bag up so Owen could see it.

While Santiago escorted the Forsberg brothers out, Detective Cochran asked, "Mr. Hunter, do you need these business owners any further?"

"No, sir."

Cochran faced them. "We appreciate you being here, but we need you all to follow Officer Santiago and give a statement about the extortion demands for protection money."

Lily, Geoff, and the Grill brothers glanced at each other then quickly filed out. As they did, the crowd outside moved closer to the window. A cluster of silver hair and purple hats lined the windows. Several picket signs clattered against the window as the women jostled for better viewing positions.

Anita Moffett, Marlene Babb, and Samuel Peyton remained along with Owen and the law enforcement officers.

Marlene looked upset by the arrest of her nephews.

Owen stepped toward Sam. "I've got a question for you."

Sam's face whitened. "Not again."

"The last time you were here. What did you find Travis playing with?"

"Who's Travis?"

Owen pointed to the cat lying in the middle of the store, its tail slowly wagging, as if it enjoyed being the center of attention.

"Oh, you mean Yerchoise," Sam muttered.

Anita mumbled, "Cat Stevens."

"Possum," said Detective Cochran.

Owen rubbed his face. *What is it with these people?* He looked back at Sam. "What was the cat playing with when you arrived last time?"

Sam's eyes drifted toward the counter. "The little Elvis head. Shameful, you ask me."

"What did you do with it when you found it?"

"I put it on the counter. I told you to have respect for the greats."

"Right."

It was subtle, and most of the guests didn't notice it, but Detective Cochran took several small steps toward Sam while he interacted with Owen.

"You liked Al, right?"

"I did," Sam said.

"He helped you out. Let you stay in his shop."

Sam's face suddenly became ashen. "Are you thinking I hurt Big Al? I could never do that, Hunter. He was my friend."

"I know, Sam." Owen put his hand on the rotund man's shoulder. "You can relax. You didn't kill Big Al."

Detective Cochran's brow furrowed. He shifted the brown paper bag from one hand to the other. He looked at Onderdonk and Ekleberry, who only shrugged in return.

"And as much as I believe Marlene disliked what Al Ferguson was doing with the local businesses, I don't believe she had the strength or the height to kill him in the manner he died."

When his words sunk in, everyone slowly turned to Anita. Her eyes widened.

Several of the protesters banged on the window. Detective Cochran glared at them until they stopped.

"But I didn't," she whispered.

"I think differently."

Anita glanced at the few remaining in the store before returning to face the big man. "How could you possibly even think that?"

"Because you brought me lunch."

"I showed you some kindness, and you accuse me of murder?"

"Since you put it that way… yeah."

Anita folded her arms over her chest. "Unbelievable."

"Not really. I couldn't figure out why you brought me a sandwich. You couldn't bring it through the front door, or all the ladies would have seen you. So you brought it to the rear door."

"You brought him lunch?" Marlene asked.

"I was being nice," Anita said. "I don't have to listen to this."

She made a move toward the front door, but Detective Cochran held up a hand. "You should stay for a minute. Hear the man out."

Anita set her jaw and glared at the cop.

"Even if you took pity on me and wanted to bring me that sandwich, the smart play would have been to deliver it at the back door then leave. No risk of anyone seeing you, but instead, you walked into my store. Do you remember?"

"Of course, I remember. I don't know why you're making such a big deal of this. I only delivered you some lunch."

"But you got down and played with Travis—"

"Cat Stevens."

"—and when you left, I realized he was playing with the head of Elvis."

"Shameful," Sam said.

"Disrespectful," Onderdonk muttered.

"I didn't think anything about it until I realized it was the wrong Elvis head. And I started putting the pieces together. Do you remember talking with me about my Elvis statue? The dancing one that the punks broke?"

"No." Anita's face reddened.

"Well, you did. And you picked the head of that statue up and examined it like it meant something to you. Probably because it did."

Roy Cochran stepped to the counter then. After placing the brown paper bag on it, he put on a pair of latex gloves. Next, he carefully extracted the headless fat Elvis statue from the bag. Then he picked up the Elvis head and settled it onto the figure.

"Fits perfect," Cochran said. The detective's eyes slid between Owen and Anita. "You two, get to explaining."

"Why would I invite everyone here, Detective, only to point out that head and implicate myself?"

Cochran stared at the porcelain statue. "You were near the cat yesterday?" he asked Anita.

"There's no proof I had anything to do with that."

"Where were you the night Al was killed?" the detective asked.

She swallowed, then said, "I was at home with my kitties."

Onderdonk glanced at Owen and tapped his watch. The big man nodded. He was out of time, but he jerked his head toward the detective and Anita. He knew he needed some help to get this across the goal line.

Ekleberry coughed slightly, and everyone looked at him. "I'm sorry, but we have to hurry this along."

"And who are you?" Anita said.

The federal agent flashed his badge. "FBI."

"Why is the FBI here?" Anita asked with wide eyes.

"Detective," Ekleberry said to Cochran, "can you pull the GPS history from her cell phone? If not, maybe we can help. She probably had it with her. And if that was the case, the phone will prove she was in the other store the night of the murder. After that, proving she was the murderer should be a slam dunk."

Detective Cochran smiled. "I like it."

Anita glanced around, her eyes growing frantic. "Self-defense," she blurted. "I hit him in self-defense."

The female officer near the front door stepped toward Anita.

Cochran clucked his tongue. "Big Al was hit on the back of the skull. I'm not sure how you claim self-defense with that but give it a try."

"Anita!" Marlene said. "How could you do such a thing?"

"I didn't mean to," she whispered. "I lost my head."

The assembled law enforcement officers groaned.

"That's not what I meant," Anita said. She held out her hands in a pleading manner. "I'd fought with Albert Ferguson for years on how to make the boardwalk a better place. When I found out he was organizing against Marlene, I went to him and asked if he needed any help. I thought maybe it was something we could find common ground on.”

“You would organize against me?” Marlene said.

“You’re not the easiest person to get along with,” Anita said. “But Al told me he didn’t want my help. He said Marlene was just a practice run. That when he was done with her, he was coming after the Business and Standards Committee. He said he was going to undo everything I’d worked so hard to accomplish. He was going to make Costa Buena great again.”

Her voice became soft, and her gaze slowly drifted toward the ground as she recalled the event.

“He demanded I get out of his store, and I lost my temper. When he turned around, I grabbed the nearest heavy thing I could find, and I hit him over the head. I didn’t think it would kill him. I didn’t want to kill him. I didn’t mean to.”

“You left the statue,” Cochran said. “We found it at the scene. But why take the Elvis head?”

Anita shrugged. “At first, I didn’t even know I had it. It must have broken off and fallen into my jacket pocket somehow. I was close to him when I... well... you know. I discovered the head when I put my clothes into the washer to... I didn’t know what to do with it. I hid it at first, knowing it was the only clue that could link me to Big Al. Then I saw that other little

Elvis head on the counter in here, and I realized what I needed to do. I put it off a couple of times until I confirmed that Mr. Owen acted exactly like Mr. Ferguson. He didn't care about the community. He only cared about himself. That's when I knew what I had to do."

Detective Roy Cochran stepped forward and grabbed Anita Moffett by the elbow. "You're under arrest for the murder of Albert Ferguson."

Chapter 40

The protesters reluctantly parted as Detective Roy Cochran escorted the handcuffed Anita Moffett through.

Women in purple hats loudly booed, and the Paws for Peace demonstrators shook their kitten photos back and forth. The female police officer waved them all back.

Sam the Scavenger and Marlene Babb stood outside the store watching it all. He had his hands tucked inside his Baja jacket. Sam said something to Marlene, and she nodded. A soft smile grew on her face. The two walked off down the boardwalk.

Watching it all from the windows were Owen Hunter, Marshal Ted Onderdonk, and FBI Agent Max Ekleberry.

With a quick check of his watch, Onderdonk said, "We've gotta go."

Owen turned to him. "Where am I headed next?"

The marshal pulled the white envelope from his rear pocket. "We've set up a—"

His words were cut off by the roar of several motorcycles thundering down the boardwalk. Outside, the protesters scattered as members of the Satan's Dawgs rode in front of the business. The three news crews all turned their cameras in the direction of the motorcycle gang.

"In the alley!" Ekleberry ordered. "I'll delay them."

The FBI man rushed out the front door as Owen and Marshal Onderdonk sprinted down the back hallway. The lawman shoved the envelope into his back pocket.

At the rear door, Owen quickly unlocked it and pushed it open.

Once outside, Owen glanced toward the opposite ends of the alley. From both directions, several motorcycles raced toward them, their engines screaming. The bikes bounced over the uneven terrain.

"Hop the fence!" the marshal yelled.

Owen took two steps and bounded the wooden fence, unaware of what might be on the other side. He landed on top of a barbecue grill, toppling it to the ground, and falling on his back.

Next to him, the marshal landed on his feet, ready to run. He reached down, grabbed Owen by the arm, and yanked him upright.

"Run!" Onderdonk hollered.

The two men sprinted southbound on Main Street. Owen's Converse shoes loudly slapped the sidewalk. He lived only five houses away, so he could see the white Toyota waiting in the small driveway.

As he ran, Owen dug the car keys from his pocket. Doing so threw off his gait, but he refused to slow.

Onderdonk slid his gun from his holster, and his eyes scanned the area for threats.

At the car, Owen unlocked it and slid behind the wheel. The engine ignited with a backfire and a plume of white smoke.

The marshal pulled the envelope from his back pocket and tossed it onto Owen's lap. "That's your new cover. Head north and call when you get somewhere safe."

"Thanks, Ted."

Onderdonk slammed the car door closed and stepped back.

The tires squealed as the Toyota reversed out of the driveway and bounced into the street. Owen dropped the car's gearshift into Drive but paused with his foot on the brake. He shook his head as he rolled down the window.

Leaning over to see the marshal better, he yelled, "Ted!"

But Onderdonk didn't look his way. He was focused on something else. Owen lifted his eyes to the rearview mirror.

Two choppers raced around the corner, their engines angrily protesting the force which their riders were demanding from them. The two men atop the bikes wore the leather vests of the Satan's Dawgs. Both had long, flowing hair. It happened so fast that Owen couldn't make out who they were.

The marshal fired two quick shots, and both bikers swerved wildly. The first bike collided with a parked pickup. The collision threw its rider into the street.

The second bike continued straight ahead, crossed into Owen's yard, and crashed into his house. The rider slipped from the bike and didn't move.

With the immediate threat neutralized, Onderdonk faced Owen and shouted, "What are you waiting for?"

Owen felt sheepish for even asking, but he said, "Don't forget my cat."

Then the big man stomped on the accelerator. A plume of white smoke shot out from the exhaust pipe.

U.S. Marshal Ted Onderdonk stood dumbfounded as the dented, white Toyota Tercel sped northbound out of Costa Buena.

Beau Smith
returns in...

Cozy Up
to Blood

FRENCH BREAD SANDWICHES

Courtesy of Meemaw

2/3 cup canned milk (not sweetened)
1½ pound hamburger
½ cup crushed crackers
½ cup diced onions
One egg
1 tbsp mustard
½ tsp seasoned salt
2 cups diced American cheese

Directions:

1. Mix all ingredients
2. Split the French bread lengthwise
3. Pile the meat mixture onto the bread but not firmly
4. Wrap the bread in aluminum foil up to the meat mixture
5. Place on a baking sheet and bake at 350 degrees for 30-35 minutes
6. Slice into pieces.

ABOUT THE AUTHOR

Besides writing the Cozy Up Series, Colin Conway is the author of the 509 Crime Stories, a series of novels set in Eastern Washington with revolving lead characters. They are standalone tales and can be read in any order.

Colin is also the co-author of the Charlie-316 series. The first book in the series, *Charlie-316*, is a political/crime thriller and has been described as "riveting and compulsively readable," "the real deal," and "the ultimate ride-along."

He served in the U.S. Army and later was an officer of the Spokane Police Department. He has owned a laundromat, invested in a bar, and run a karate school. Besides writing crime fiction, he is a commercial real estate broker.

Colin lives with his beautiful girlfriend, three wonderful children, and a codependent Vizsla that rules their world.

Find out more at colinconway.com.